HURRICANE
SEASON

HURRICANE SEASON

Mickey Friedman

A JOAN KAHN BOOK

E. P. DUTTON, INC. New York

There is a town in Florida named Palmetto. It is not in the northwest part of the state, and the author has never visited it. The Palmetto in this story, and its inhabitants, are entirely fictional and bear no relation to a real place or real people.

Published in the United States by E. P. Dutton, Inc., 2 Park Avenue, New York, N.Y. 10016

Library of Congress Cataloging in Publication Data

Friedman, Mickey.
    Hurricane season.
    "A Joan Kahn Book."
    I. Title.
PS3556.R53H8   1983   813'.54   82-14645

ISBN: 0-525-24175-2

Copyedited by Lorraine Alexander Veach

10 9 8 7 6 5 4 3 2 1

First Edition

Design by Stanley S. Drate

To Alan

HURRICANE
SEASON

Prologue
Hurricane Season:
Palmetto, Florida, 1952

Hurricane season comes when the year is exhausted. In the damp, choking heat of August and September, the days go on forever to no purpose. Hurricanes linger in the back of the mind as a threat and a promise. The threat is the threat of destruction. The promise is that something could happen, that the air could stir and become clammy, the heat could lift, the bay start to wallow like a huge humpbacked animal.

If a hurricane came, there would be something to do besides drink iced tea on the front porch and take long, sweat-soaked naps in the afternoon; there would be something to talk about besides how hot it is. So hurricanes linger in the back of the mind.

Palmetto is in northwest Florida on a corner of land that juts into the Gulf of Mexico. Tourists bound for Miami, or Palm Beach, or Fort Lauderdale do not see Palmetto or know about it. In their rush to the south, they do not pass near it. They want palm trees and hibiscus; Palmetto has scrub oak, and miles of sawgrass through which salt streams meander, and acres of pine woods. It has broad, slow-moving brown rivers lined with cypress swamps.

Water is a presence, and people live in connection with it. They fish, or deal in oysters, scallops, and shrimp. On the beach road, there are fisheries built on pilings over the water, corrugated iron oyster shacks, shrimp boats with

1

swathes of net. People travel by boat where the roads don't go—across the bay to St. Elmo's Island or down the sloughs deep into the river swamp.

The beaches near Palmetto are wide and white, unmarked except for the curving line of the sea wrack. Jerry-built piers, weathered to soft gray, stagger into the bay, and on them an occasional fisherman flicks a line.

About seven miles out of town, opposite one of these piers—a pier bigger and more sturdy than some—is a low concrete-block structure. A sagging wooden telephone booth leans near the corner of the building, and two pumps of Gulf gas stand under the breezeway in front. Metal signs, rusting in the salt air, advertise *Ice, Live Bait, Fresh Sweet Honey, Coca-Cola*. Above the door, in faded blue letters, is written *Trulock's Grocery & Marine Supply*. This is the landing where the ferry *Island Queen* docks three times a day on its trips back and forth to St. Elmo's Island. The store, and the house across the road where Lily and Aubrey Trulock live, are St. Elmo's Landing.

Across the bay, a dark green line on the horizon, is St. Elmo's Island. During the twenties St. Elmo was a resort, with a reputation that spread as far away as Atlanta and Birmingham. There was a boardwalk and a hotel, the Elmo House, with gingerbread trim and red-and-white striped awnings, and a seawater pool near the ocean.

The great days of St. Elmo were brief and have been over a long time. The Elmo House is boarded up, loosening at the joints in the wind and blowing sand. Adventurous lovers and beer-drinking teenagers have found their way inside and left crude messages. The pool, drained long ago, now contains only sand, occasional rainwater, dried seaweed, discarded egg cases from marine creatures.

The Elmo House sags nearer to the earth. Every year, people wonder if it will survive another hurricane season.

The Womanless Wedding

In August 1952, the Palmetto Men's Lodge put on a Womanless Wedding. The lodge members had talked about other ways of raising money—a talent show, a fish fry—but these were rejected. Donald La Grange, whose tap dancing was always the hit of any Palmetto talent show (especially the finale to "Swanee") was laid up after twisting an ankle chasing his bird dog through the woods. As for a fish fry, the men thought soon everybody would be fish-fried out, it being an election year. There hadn't been a Womanless Wedding in Palmetto since '48, when Eldred Segrist ruined everything by setting his wig on fire with one of the candles. It was time for another.

Ticket sales were brisk at fifty cents apiece. The Palmetto Elementary School auditorium would be full. Although he had vowed never to do it again after what had happened the last time, Luke Draper agreed to sing his falsetto "O Promise Me." And despite his reelection campaign against a strong challenge by LeRoy ("Gospel Roy") McInnes, the First Baptist choir director, Congressman Robert ("Snapper") Landis agreed to be the preacher.

The preacher was a good role for Snapper. It was fairly dignified, since he wouldn't have to mess around with wigs and falsies; but he'd also get to use his politician's voice and might even get to work some words about the Communist Threat into the invocation.

3

On the evening of the performance, people gathered in the sandy schoolyard, avoiding the heat of indoors. Teen-aged girls in freshly ironed sundresses giggled and eyed the teenaged boys draped over parked cars. Children, oblivious to the heat, screamed and chased each other while their mothers watched languidly. Men greeted each other with uneasy camaraderie and talked about the frogs they'd gigged the last time they'd gone frogging, or how many squirrels they'd shot recently.

Male laughter drifted from the lighted classroom where the wedding's cast was getting into costume. With the onset of deep dusk, the mosquitos got bad and drove everyone indoors.

Lily and Aubrey Trulock arrived while the crowd was trooping into the auditorium. The room was filled with the slapping sound of hard wooden seats being folded down. At either end of the stage, in front of the threadbare red curtain, were white florists' baskets filled with balloons. Lily hadn't much wanted to come, she told herself. It was, after all, seven miles in and seven miles back to the Landing. But Aubrey was a lodge member, even though he hadn't been to the meetings (or much of anywhere else, except his apiary) since his heart attack. He hadn't said anything, but Lily believed he wanted to come, and since he'd been willing to walk out and get in the car, she supposed she was right.

Now that they were here, though, she felt irritated. Instead of going down to the first two rows of seats, where his lodge buddies were waiting to cheer on their fellows, Aubrey hung back and sat meekly by her in the middle of the auditorium.

"There's Jack. Don't you want to see Jack?" asked Lily, fanning herself with her church fan, a cardboard picture of Jesus Risen from the Tomb stapled to a wooden stick. She glared at his perspiring pink forehead as, eyes downcast, he shrugged. "I expect Jack would like to see *you*," she said.

When she got no response she craned her head around to survey the crowd.

Lily liked to keep up with what was happening. She was a wiry woman in her mid-fifties. Her skin was dark brown and roughened by years of exposure to the coastal sun, her light green eyes surrounded by wrinkles from squinting in the glare. She could run a boat, pump gas, open oysters. She had more energy than it took to keep a store, and she used it to stay abreast of events.

Wesley Stafford was across the way, she saw, standing slightly apart from a crowd of Methodist youth. Wesley, a ministerial student from Montgomery who had worked with the young people for the summer, looked ill at ease. His companions seemed to be cracking jokes among themselves and ignoring him. She had known from the beginning, Lily told herself, that Wesley was too gawky and intense to make an impression on the youth, since they had been spoiled last year by a young music minister who played the banjo. Something about Wesley—with the short sleeves of his shirt flapping around his thin arms, his hair wildly cowlicked, his eyes behind glasses fixed in a nervous stare—reminded Lily of the flamingo on a postcard her friend Theo had sent her from Miami once. Wesley's elbows, she realized, looked like that flamingo's knees.

Wesley's gaze was fixed on the back of the room. Twisting her head, Lily saw Diana Landis slouching against the back wall of the auditorium. Lily clucked. "Snapper's girl is here," she whispered to Aubrey, and turned to look again. Diana had never dressed in a manner appropriate to a congressman's daughter. Tonight she had on shorts and a peasant blouse that seemed to be a little too large, since it was slipping off one shoulder. Her hair was a tangle of black curls around her sullen-looking olive-skinned face. It was a mystery to Lily why the men kept after her the way they did. Maybe it was her wild reputation.

Diana could be trusted to embarrass her father if she

possibly could. She had undoubtedly lost him votes in the churches, where Gospel Roy was making the most of it. But if Diana had lost Snapper votes in the churches, it was possible she'd made up for it in the bars, where her acquaintance was widest. Most of Palmetto, it seemed to Lily, swore by one or the other institution.

Gospel Roy had been out to Trulock's Grocery & Marine Supply to discuss the matter. "I'm not one to talk about a man's kin," he'd said, leaning so close Lily had smelled the Vitalis on his wavy gray hair. "But I say, a state congressman has to set an example. When you got a weak link. . . . Well, Joe McCarthy's been showing us what can happen when you got a weak link." (Of Gospel Roy's six children, one was a football star at Auburn, one was a lay preacher, and all the rest sang in the First Baptist choir.)

It hadn't occurred to Lily that Diana Landis might be part of the International Communist Conspiracy, but she supposed she could see some logic in it. Diana *was* a weak link where men were concerned, and any male International Communist who visited Palmetto could probably get well acquainted with her without too much effort. The best Lily could think of to do was give Roy a free NuGrape and say, "I don't know, Roy, I got to have time to think it over." And with that Roy had had to be satisfied.

The thwack of flesh on flesh interrupted Lily's reverie. She turned to find Aubrey swaying, after a slap on the back from Snapper himself, who was wearing the red galluses and gaudy ascot of his preacher costume. Snapper's blue eyes were bright in his ruddy face, and his slicked-back hair, Lily thought, looked suspiciously blacker than it had when he in his turn had been out at the store calling Gospel Roy "a good man—don't get me wrong, Miss Lily—but being able to blow a pitch pipe and wave your hands around while a congregation sings 'Rock of Ages' ain't a qualification for the state congress."

"How you doing, young fella?" he said to Aubrey.

Aubrey pinkened. "What say, you snapping turtle?"

"What's this I hear about you being laid up?"

"Heart attack last year."

"You take care, now. Don't let them bees get the best of you, old son," said Snapper, his eyes sweeping the crowd. He winked at Lily. "Miss Lily, you look after my young friend here. Don't let him get bee stung." Before Lily could speak, he was off down the aisle, waving to someone else. Aubrey, Lily noticed, was still flushed with pleasure.

"Nice of Snapper," Lily said.

"He's a fine old boy," said Aubrey, and Lily realized how seldom these days she heard him volunteer an opinion.

"You should go on down and speak to your friends," she said, but Aubrey had lapsed into his usual uncommunicative state, eyes downcast and hands lying limply on his knees.

It was time to begin, anyway. Behind a screen down front Cora Baker, the only woman participant—no man in Palmetto knew how to play the piano—launched into "The Wedding March." A few giggles rippled across the auditorium, and the Womanless Wedding was under way.

Afterward, when the fuss had died down, many Palmetto residents said the wedding had started out the best they'd ever seen. The parade of bridesmaids—each flinging "her" false curls about and daintily holding up skirts made of everything from red velvet winter curtains to croker sacks—had been better than ever. At the height of it, one of the balloons stuffed in Otis Walker's blouse burst, and the laughter as half his bosom flattened could have been heard on St. Elmo's Island.

Snapper stole the show as the preacher. He clowned, forgot his lines, and worked the names of prominent Palmetto citizens into the service. He pinched several bridesmaids on the behind, and J. D. Lyons, the matron of honor, hit him with J. D.'s wife's beaded reticule. When the father of the bride marched down the aisle carrying his shotgun over his shoulder, Snapper brought down the house by trying to hide beneath the pulpit and then behind the bridesmaids' skirts.

Then came the bride—Jasper Middleton, weighing two hundred fifty pounds at least, wearing a lace tablecloth for a veil. Jasper's painted lips were pursed, he had a beauty mark on his cheek, and he minced along blowing kisses to the crowd, his hairy arms straining the seams on a pair of mitts his mother had crocheted especially for the occasion.

At just that high point, all hell broke loose. Over the laughter that greeted Jasper's progress down the aisle, a hoarse and desperate-sounding voice cried from the back of the auditorium, "Help! Come help! The swamp is on fire!" and Bo Calhoun, his face and clothes smoke-stained, pushed past Jasper to the front of the auditorium.

Lily thought at first that Bo's entrance, ill-timed as it was, was part of the show, perhaps some sort of blackface interlude. It took her a second or two to realize that Bo wasn't even a member of the lodge. And when he raced past her, she smelled smoke on his clothes and saw sweat and what looked very much like tears, although this was hard to credit, on his face.

Probably more than half the audience, when they heard Bo say the swamp was on fire, knew he meant his family's moonshine still, the biggest in the county. Bo hadn't reached the stage before many were on their feet. One of the wedding party—the fire chief, who was playing the mother of the bride, wearing a mop for a wig, started to run, stepped on the hem of his long skirt, and fell to his knees, knocking the mop askew. "You watch out, Harold! That's Mama's Eastern Star dress!" screamed his wife from her seat in the third row.

"The swamp's on fire!" Bo yelled again. He glanced around wildly and ran back up the aisle.

By this time, people were heading for the doors. Jasper,

the bride, who hadn't quite reached the stage when Bo arrived, dropped his bouquet of baby's breath into someone's lap, yelled, "You-all come *on!*" charged up the aisle in Bo's wake. This galvanized the rest of the wedding party, which, grabbing off wigs and pulling up skirts to expose hairy legs and feet shoved into high heels, stumbled after him.

The casualties, totted up later, were not serious: several broken shoe heels, a bottle of bourbon smashed when it fell out of a flower arrangement, a sprained wrist, and a broken collarbone resulting from a fall off the stage. The stage was clear inside of ten minutes and the auditorium was half-empty. Somebody had the presence of mind to pull the curtain, and Cora Baker struck up the recessional.

Lily had no trouble figuring out what had happened. Bo had discovered the fire at the family's still, and—failing to rouse the volunteer fire department, or knowing in the first place nobody would be there—had come to the place where he could summon the most manpower the quickest.

"Guess the Calhouns' still blew up," she said to Aubrey. From outside came the sound of tires screeching. A few remaining members of the wedding party milled about. The "country cousin" removed flaxen braids and scrubbed morosely at blacked-out front teeth, and one of the bridesmaids mopped his face with a lace hankie.

"My Law'," said the woman sitting next to Lily. "It sure does look like to me they better do a minstrel show next time."

Lily stood up and beckoned to Aubrey. "We might as well go on home," she said. "I reckon that does it for another Womanless Wedding."

A Proposal

"What time is it?" asked Bo Calhoun.

He was standing in the tiny cabin of Diana Landis's boat in his undershorts. He was a powerfully built man with auburn hair, freckles across his nose and shoulders, and a bony face.

It was two days after the Calhoun family moonshine operation had been destroyed by a fire that, the Calhouns agreed among themselves, had been started by dynamite. They had had enough stills dynamited by the law to know the signs. This time, though, it hadn't been the law.

"You hear me?" Bo said.

The cabin had a bunk on one wall, a counter with fishing equipment strewn over it on the other. Diana Landis lay naked on the bunk, her elbow crooked over her eyes. "Oh my God," she said.

"Don't start up," said Bo. "I asked you a question."

Diana removed her elbow and turned her head toward him. "You want to know what time it is? I'll tell you what time it is," she said. "It's time you did something about this situation, that's what time it is."

"Didn't I ask you not to start up?"

"You don't understand." Diana sat up, huddled in a corner of the bunk. "I love you, Bo."

Bo didn't move.

"Things are different now. It's a lot more important now," she said. "There may be reasons why I have to get out of town." Her voice shook on the last words, and she put her hand over her mouth.

"What are you talking about?" Bo walked to the bunk and sat down.

Diana slid near him. "I can't tell you," she said. "I just have to be with you. You told me how mean Sue Nell is, and how I make you happy. Now I need you, really bad."

Bo picked up cigarettes and matches from the floor beside the bunk and lit up, squinting against the smoke. "Have you done something?"

She pounded the bunk with her fist. "What if I have? Why should you be with that ugly, red-headed bitch and not with me?"

His upraised hand moved swiftly toward her face, but in the end he simply grasped her chin and shoved it to one side. "Watch out," he said.

Diana's eyes were red. "Please tell her, Bo."

"Tell me what you did."

She shook her head. "Nothing. Nothing. I just want to be with you so much, and now. . . ." She bent her head.

Bo looked at her. His face changed. He put his arm around her shoulders and drew her close. Minutes passed before he said, "I can't do it, Miss Di."

She shuddered but said nothing. At last she said, "Not today. But soon."

He didn't respond. Burying his hand in her hair, he said, "Did you write me another poem?"

She nodded.

"Read it to me while I get my clothes on?"

While he put on khaki pants and buttoned his shirt, she read from a school composition book:

> The hot rain pounds the sandy shore,
> The gulls shriek in the sky.
> The smothering air can harm me less
> Than knowing I have to lie.

"That's real nice . . ." Bo began soothingly, but Diana cut him off:

> I have to share what can't be shared
> Forget what ought to be.
> The gulls may scream for grief or loss—

her voice choked—

> I think they scream for me.

Diana sat swallowing and blinking, her eyes fixed on the book.

"Now, that's mighty pretty," said Bo. "How you can make those rhymes I just don't know." He raised her face to his and kissed her. "I got to go."

Diana listened to his footsteps fade out along the dock. She sat on the bunk a long time before starting to get dressed.

Labor Day

By Labor Day, Palmetto had almost stopped talking about Bo Calhoun's interruption of the Womanless Wedding and the destruction of the Calhoun family still. The elections were taking a lot of attention. Snapper and Gospel Roy sniped at each other daily, and on the national scene Palmetto was wondering whether to vote for Eisenhower or Stevenson.

"I feel bound to warn you that you will have trouble getting votes down in this part of the country," Lily Trulock wrote to Adlai Stevenson. "But it is still my belief that once a Democrat always a Democrat." She enclosed two dollars in the envelope. Other Palmetto citizens, however, planned a motorcade up to Birmingham to hear Ike speak on September third.

When anyone did mention the Calhouns' still, it was to wonder where they'd build it next time. The Calhouns had been making whiskey in the swamp for as long as anyone could remember. Each of the four Calhoun boys drove a late-model Oldsmobile, and before the tragedy they had been going to Georgia with a load once a week. Anyone who knew could spot them on the highway. Bo would be driving lead, Sonny with the load—a trunk and specially constructed back seat full of five-gallon demijohns (the Calhouns called them "jimmy johns")—Lester on the tail, and Purvis on shotgun, to decoy the law.

13

Purvis's job was to drive erratically and fast, so that if the highway patrol was around they'd find him more interesting than his brothers, who observed the speed limit strictly. The system worked well, with only an occasional speeding ticket for Purvis.

Although the law, including County Sheriff Woody Malone, had been out to fight the fire, and it was obvious that the barrels and cookers going up in flames were a setup for moonshine, nobody had felt it worthwhile to prosecute the Calhoun brothers. In the first place, the Calhouns were generous contributors to Sheriff Malone's reelection campaigns, and also, if a deer happened to wander across their property and one of them shot it, the sheriff always got a quarter of it for his freezer.

It was over a Labor Day dinner of barbecued venison that the sheriff confided to his wife's parents, Lily and Aubrey Trulock, that Bo Calhoun suspected the still had been sabotaged. "It could of just exploded, of course," he said, helping himself to more yams. "Bo was on his way there, but he said he heard it go boom, boom, boom, just like that and up she went. It was like dynamite was set at three different places. Stop that bubbling, Junior, or I'll take a strap to you."

"What do you plan to do about it?" asked Lily.

Woody smirked. "There isn't much I can do to somebody for destroying an illegal still, Mother Trulock. It's what I would've done myself, if I'd found it first."

Lily hated to be called "Mother Trulock," and she suspected Woody knew it. "I suppose the Calhouns are mad."

"Yes, ma'am, I reckon they are. Bo says if he catches who did it—"

"Can't we talk about something more suitable for a family dinner?" put in Wanda, the Trulocks' daughter. "More venison, Daddy?"

Lily ignored her. "He'll what?"

"Fill his rear full of buckshot, at the very least. Probably worse. Wanda, that was mighty fine. I'm full as a tick."

Lily cleared away the dishes while Wanda sliced lemon meringue pie. "Who would want to blow up the Calhouns' still?" Lily asked Woody, who was picking his teeth with the corner of a cardboard matchbook.

"I sure don't know, Mother Trulock," he said, his voice muffled. He removed the matchbook and continued, "I think maybe Bo was just upset. He flies off the handle easy."

Lily had just sold Bo Calhoun a new cast net. She had also persuaded him to buy a mold for making lead weights for the net. The mold was uneven, but he had taken it for only fifty cents off. Therefore, she was inclined to be sympathetic. "It's a bad thing to have your livelihood taken away," she said. "Not that I hold with drinking any kind of liquor."

"I should *hope* not," came Wanda's voice from the kitchen.

"Did you ever taste moonshine, Aubrey?" asked Lily.

Aubrey looked at the tablecloth. "Naw," he said.

"It ain't that special," said Woody. "But I tell you, since the liquor taxes went up last year they are purely selling a bunch of it. With that ten-fifty tax on a gallon of legal whiskey, the government thought they were going to get a whole mess of money. Instead, they just put the moonshiners in high cotton. The government is making less off liquor now that it did before taxes went up, because everybody's buying moonshine instead." He belched. "It don't make my job any easier," he added as a pious afterthought.

"The government is working as well as it usually does," said Lily. "Who do you like for president?"

"Ike," said Woody promptly.

"No need to make up your mind right yet," said Lily. "There's still plenty of time till election day."

"Pie and politics don't mix," said Wanda. "Sit up straight, Junior. It's time for dessert."

On the Island

On the evening of Labor Day, Joshua Burns was crossing the bay from the mainland to St. Elmo's Island. He sat in the back of the open boat, his hand on the tiller of the outboard motor, while a sluggish breeze ballooned his sweat-stained shirt and lifted the dark hair from his forehead.

Josh knew he could be picked out from shore, silhouetted in the reflection the setting sun cast on the water, but he felt reasonably sure nobody was interested. The grocery store at St. Elmo's Landing was closed, and that was the only inhabited location for a couple of miles down the coast except for the summer cottages, which either were closed for the winter or housed outsiders who wouldn't wonder.

As the boat drew closer to St. Elmo, he could see the ruined hotel, the Elmo House, outlined against the dunes. He veered away from it. The north end of St. Elmo was not his destination. Not much of the island, he had gathered in his short acquaintance with it, had ever been inhabited. The few miles of white sand beach at the north end had drawn visitors, and it was near the beach that St. Elmo's inhabitants still lived, in a cluster of concrete-block bungalows. Most of the island was untouched, with its thick pine woods and tangled undergrowth, its perimeters lined with sawgrass to the water's edge.

Josh guided his boat toward this less hospitable part of St. Elmo. Now, he easily recognized the features of the island's

16

coastline that were his signposts. Opening the throttle wide, he swung around the southern tip of the island. Seeing the wide-open Gulf gave him the lightheaded feeling he always got at that moment.

His eyes swept the darkening shore, searching for the ragged, outsize clump of yucca that marked the entrance to the channel. The channel had been one of his tests. "Reckon you can maneuver a boat through there without knocking the bottom off it?" Murphy had asked.

Josh had looked and said, "I reckon so," and had taken the vibrating tiller when Murphy wordlessly handed it over. The temptation had been to show off, but that wasn't Josh's style. He carefully took the boat through the almost unnoticeable break in the sawgrass and up the narrow channel under the pine boughs.

Now that Josh thought of it, the episode hadn't really been a test. By the time he and Murphy had gotten that far, they both knew he was going to go to work. The tricky part had been earlier, when he was pumping gas at the fuel station on the canal where Murphy came to gas up his cabin cruiser.

"I ain't seen you here before," Murphy had said, drinking an R.C. while Josh hooked up the hose.

"No sir," Josh had said.

"You from this part of the world?"

Josh shook his head. "Close to Columbus."

"Georgia boy, eh? What you doing down here?"

"Looking for something to make me some money—a job, I guess,"

Murphy finished his drink and put it in the weathered wooden crate leaning against the boathouse. "You know anything about boats?"

"Some. Pretty good bit."

That was all the conversation the first time. But Murphy had returned, and each visit Josh had been conscious of the man's watching him with his small eyes, slapping the side of

his gut his shirt would barely button over. His conversa-
tions with Josh always got around to two matters: the fact
that Josh didn't know many people in Palmetto, and Josh's
need for money.

"Got a girl, have you?" Murphy asked once, his lips
sinking deeper in the flesh of his cheeks.

"Sort of."

"Lives up there in Columbus?"

"Yessir."

"What's the matter with her, let a fine young man like you
run off down here?"

"Her mama don't like poor boys."

"Ain't that the way," said Murphy, sounding satisfied.

It was on Murphy's next visit that he told Josh he might
have a job for him. "I don't know what you're making,
jockeying these here pumps, but I imagine I can do better.
Are you interested?"

"Sure I am," said Josh.

They arranged to meet that evening at Sal's Roadhouse,
and while Johnnie Ray sobbed "The Little White Cloud
That Cried" on the jukebox, Murphy quizzed him. Why
wasn't he fighting in Korea? Why did he come to Palmetto
to look for work? What kind of jobs had he done before?

Josh answered stolidly. He'd tried to sign up but had a
heart murmur. He'd come to Palmetto because he'd gotten
a ride this far. He grew up on a farm, and had done a lot of
jobs, but was best at mechanical things—working on boats,
cars, and such.

Murphy ran a thick forefinger down the side of his beer
bottle and said, "What's your feeling about corn liquor,
son?"

Josh shrugged, "One time when I was fifteen, my brother
and I drank up some my daddy had, and he gave us a
whipping for it."

Murphy grunted. "Making it's against the law, you
know."

"So is fishing without a license, but that ain't stopped me from pulling in many a bream without paying no two dollars."

Murphy nodded, and the next day Josh quit his job and went to work for Murphy.

The grass was still burnished by the setting sun, but once into the woods it was dimmer, the sandy banks of the channel level with his head. He put-putted around the turns, waving once to a blond man wearing overalls and holding a shotgun, who was leaning against a tree. As he rounded a bend, he noticed the sourish smell that mingled with the scent of the water and the pines.

A dock made of raw, unweathered lumber jutted into the water, hung with old tires to keep tied-up boats from scraping against it. Josh drifted in, picked up a string of fish from the bottom of the boat, jumped from the bow to the dock, and tied up. Murphy emerged from the underbrush and said, "Where you been, boy? We needed you an hour ago."

Josh held up the fish. "They started biting. Thought you might like some for supper."

Murphy nodded and led the way along a rudimentary path to a clearing. Here, the last rays of the sun revealed barrels, vats, copper tubing, kerosene cans. The smell hung in the unmoving air. A shed stood on one side of the clearing, and outside it a bristly-haired young man was lighting a lantern. He adjusted the wick and hung it from a nail outside the door, over a small makeshift shelf that held a camp stove. Josh held up his string of fish again. "Suppertime," he said. "Time to get the grits on." A few minutes later, the blond sentry Josh had passed on the way in arrived.

After their meal, the smell of fried fish and hush puppies lingering, it was dark enough to begin the night's work. Josh slipped on his headlamp, a light like a miner's that was meant to be used for frogging, blinding frogs at night so you could stick them with a gig. It had the advantage of leaving the hands free to pass wooden cases and load them into the boat.

When one boat was loaded and sitting low in the water, Josh and Murphy took the other down the channel. Josh's headlight picked out the curves of the bank, occasionally flashing in the eyes of a possum or a coon. Once in the ocean, they could feel that the wind had picked up slightly, and it sent a sultry breath across the bow. Five minutes' ride took them tó the inlet, hidden to the casual passerby, where Murphy's cabin cruiser was anchored. Murphy got aboard, started the engine, and followed Josh back to the mouth of the channel where the other two men were waiting with the loaded boat. Josh left Murphy and the blond sentry to transfer cartons while he and the bristly-haired man returned for another load. It took them an hour, rotating, to get the cruiser loaded.

"That's all she wrote," said Josh, wiping his forehead on his sleeve.

Murphy checked his watch. "The truck'll be there in an hour. I'll see you boys tomorrow. We run again the day after."

"Tomorrow's payday, right?" asked Josh.

"That's right," said Murphy shortly.'

Josh swung over the side of Murphy's boat and landed in his own. The men rode back to the dock in silence, as the sound of Murphy's motor died in the distance.

When they disembarked, however, Josh said, "Close bastard, ain't he?"

"Don't you worry about it," said the blond man.

"Promises all kind of things, but you don't see the color of his money very often."

"That's true for sure," said the bristly-haired man.

The blond man turned swiftly on the bristly one. "What are you worried about, Larry?"

"Nothing, Amos," said Larry hastily.

Josh said, "It would be teetotally too bad if this turned out to be for nothing. Murphy talks a lot, and he drives a big old boat, but have we got to wait till he sells that liquor before we see any money? That could be another week or more."

"I told you don't worry about it," said Amos.

"You didn't tell me why not," said Josh.

The three reached the clearing. In the feeble lantern light, Amos entered the shed and emerged with a fruit jar of clear liquid. He unscrewed the top, sipped, and held it out to Josh. Josh sipped and felt the sensation, familiar now, that the front of his skull had been blown away. Lord, I hate this stuff, he thought.

"There's plenty money behind this here operation," Amos said while Larry drank.

"Yeah? Whose?" said Josh.

"Murphy don't say. But you'll get paid tomorrow. Wait and see."

Josh took another swallow from the jar, handed it on, and opened the door of the shed. The air inside was hot and still. He could just make out the three cots in the dimness. "Reckon I'll have to do that, being there's nothing else I can do," he said, yawning.

"You ain't planning to go to sleep now, are you?" said Amos. "You're on sentry duty till two."

Without a word, Josh picked up the shotgun from where it was propped next to the door and strode off through the woods. He was tired and dizzy. A mosquito buzzed in his ear. He wished, and not for the first time, that he'd never left Georgia.

Pearl and Diana

Pearl Washington walked through the backyard, past the azalea bushes, and climbed the back steps of Congressman Snapper Landis's house. It was eight o'clock in the morning when she let herself in the door, early enough to feel some of night's fugitive coolness.

Snapper's house was on the edge of town, on land not long since reclaimed from dunes. The place had been fairly recently built, with—rumor had it—generous help from Snapper's friends and constituents who were contractors, plumbers, and roofers. Its raw pink brick belied their efforts to re-create the Old South. The white columns on the front porch were too skinny, and the white rocking chairs on the veranda looked stickily new and had obviously never been sat in.

Where Pearl lived, in one of a huddle of shacks called Bacon's Settlement, built on sandy earth near the canal, the days started early. Babies fretted, a draggle-tailed rooster crowed as if he had something to be proud of, and feet hit the plank floors inside the close, tin-roofed cabins that never cooled off in summer and were never warm in winter.

Once inside the Landis house, Pearl took off her shoes and put on the house slippers she kept in the broom closet under the hook where she hung her apron. She was a large woman and on her feet most of the day. The Landis household was still. That was good. If Snapper wanted his coffee before Pearl arrived, he got mad if she wasn't there to make it for him. Sometimes she found him in the kitchen, in undershirt and trousers, hair awry. "God dog it, Pearl," he would say when she came in, "look at the mess I've made because I wanted me some coffee."

After thirteen years as a widower, Snapper could fix himself a cup of coffee, Pearl knew. Hands on hips, she would survey the scene—spilled coffee grounds, pieces of the percolator spread over the counter top—knowing it had been done for her benefit. "It's a mess all right," she would say, and Snapper, secure in moral victory, would let her get on with cleaning it up.

Today, Pearl had the coffee perked and the grits made, and still the only sound was a mockingbird in the mimosa tree outside the kitchen window. She poured coffee into a china cup with pink roses around the rim and, balancing it carefully on its saucer, climbed the stairs.

Snapper's bedroom door was open, and Pearl peeked in. A pair of antlers with a shirt hanging from one prong and a rack of shotguns decorated the walls. The bed was empty and unmade. He had been gone a lot lately. Maybe it was something to do with the election. But it wasn't for him she'd climbed the stairs. She moved down the hall to another door, this one closed, tapped lightly, and opened it.

Diana was asleep, the pink-sprigged bedspread bunched around her knees.

Her naked body, the small round breasts with deep pink nipples, the black pubic hair, contrasted with the frilly pink-and-white organdy little-girlishness of the room. The innocent decor was also at odds with the ashtray overflowing with cigarette butts. The clothes she had worn yesterday were heaped in a corner in a way that meant they had been kicked there. Despite the oscillating fan, the air in the room was sour.

Pearl crossed the room, put the coffee on the nightstand, and sat on the edge of the bed. "Good morning, precious," she said.

Diana grimaced, moaned, and turned away. Pearl rested her hand on Diana's hair. "Come on, Miss Di. I brought you a cup of coffee."

Diana wrinkled her nose and put her hands over her face. Her hands were small, almost child-size, the nails bitten down. She pressed the heels of her palms against her eyes.

Pearl proffered the coffee. After a few moments, Diana removed her hands, squinted, and slid to half-prop herself against the headboard. She took the coffee, sipped, and shuddered. "Ugh," she said.

"You have a bad time last evening?"

She shuddered again. "None of your business."

Pearl accepted this in silence. In a few moments, Diana's face crumpled and tears seeped out of her eyes. "He doesn't love me, Pearl," she said.

"Now, sugar."

"I swear, he just plain hates me."

"He don't hate you."

"He does." Diana took a swallow of coffee and turned her wet face to Pearl. "He almost hit me. He had his arm up."

"Why'd he do it?"

"I said something nasty about his wife."

"There, you see? He was just upset."

"He hates me." Diana's voice carried less conviction now.

Pearl got up, picked up the clothes from the floor, and started to hang them in the closet. "Where's your daddy this morning?"

Diana fished a pack of Camels from the nightstand drawer, drew out a cigarette, and lit it. "Who cares? If we're lucky, maybe he drowned in the swamp."

"That's not nice, Miss Di."

"Well, I don't know where he is."

Pearl shook out a black lace half-slip, folded it, and put it in a dresser drawer. Diana took the composition book from the nightstand drawer and ran her hand over the cover. "He liked my last poem, though. The one about 'The gulls scream in the sky'? He said it was real pretty."

"There, you see?" said Pearl.

Diana made a snuffling sound. "I've been bad, Pearl," she said.

"Oh, sugar." Pearl crossed to the bed and sat next to Diana. Her voice took on a dreamy tone. "You were about the sweetest little girl I ever did see. And when your mama was taken, Mr. Snapper said to me, 'Pearl, you got to help me look after that poor motherless—' "

"Oh, Pearl!" Diana sobbed. Pearl put her arm around Diana's shoulders.

"No use getting this way over a man."

Diana sobbed louder. "The awful things I've done. All for him. And he treats me like this!"

"A man will do it. Every time."

They sat until Diana's crying lessened. She lay back against the pillows. "I'll be down to breakfast soon."

As Pearl put the bacon in the skillet and got out the eggs, she thought about Diana. Diana had turned out to be a wild girl. She had acted up all through high school—drinking, skipping classes, running around with men from the Coast Guard station—and without Snapper's intervention she wouldn't have graduated.

Now that she was out of school, she was worse. Pearl heard jokes about her around town, sly remarks about her ways. Pearl's neighbors in Bacon's Settlement, who knew everything about Palmetto's white population, shook their heads when Pearl tried to defend Diana. To them, Diana was simply no 'count and trashy. Pearl could have told them, but didn't, telling only her daughter, Marinda, that Diana could also be mean as a snake, would throw her hairbrushes across the room, and scream and curse at Pearl and her daddy.

"What are you studying her for, then?" Marinda asked, her eyes hard.

"You ask me that? You two girls used to play with her doll dishes in Mr. Snapper's backyard."

"That don't give her leave to throw no brushes."

Pearl knew Marinda was right. But the truth was, whenever she saw or heard about Diana getting drunk or making a fool of herself with some man, she didn't see the Diana of twenty, but an eight-year-old Diana sitting on Snapper's front steps with her arms wound around her knees on the afternoon they told her her mother was dead. "You must be a grown-up girl now and look after your daddy," Pearl had heard one of the church ladies say to the motionless child.

"I went to get her then, and she was cold as a fish's belly. I stood her up and she wet her pants," Pearl told Marinda.

Marinda picked up her crawling son from the floor and balanced him on her knee.

"The poor child," Pearl persisted, and Marinda glanced around at the dingy little room where the two women and the baby sat next to the oil stove.

Now, Diana was mixed up with a new man who was married. That was Diana's luck. She had used a lot of men and they'd used her, but the one she was really sweet on had to be married.

Pearl had just poured the eggs into the sizzling pan when Diana appeared. Aside from the redness at the tip of her nose, no trace of her tears remained. She wore red shorts, a halter top, and sandals, and her hair was combed. Her eyes flicked over Pearl as if she barely recognized her, and she flung herself into a chair at the kitchen table without speaking.

She nibbled her breakfast while Pearl, at the sink, got started on the dishes.

After a few minutes, Diana stood up. "I'm not putting up with it any longer," she said.

Pearl looked over her shoulder. "With what?"

"Any of it. Any of it."

"Sugar, don't—"

"I mean it, Pearl. You watch and see."

She turned and left the house. From the window, Pearl saw her run across the yard to the garage and a minute or two later heard the motor of her car. She saw a flash of chrome as Diana drove away. Then she turned back to the dishes.

A Choice

When Diana arrived, Sue Nell Calhoun was sitting in her front porch swing mending a net. Although everyone knew the Calhouns made their living from moonshine, they were supposedly fishermen, owners of one boat that left the dock only often enough to keep up an impression of activity. While Diana picked her way through the sandspurs in the Calhouns' yard, Sue Nell put down her shuttle and gauge board and watched without getting up.

Sue Nell had long red hair that frizzed in the damp. She wore it pulled to the back of her neck with a rubber band. She was freckled and almost as tall as her husband, Bo. Their resemblance to one another was natural, since they were third cousins. In the Calhoun family, Sue Nell had a reputation for being sharp-tongued and standoffish, and even Old Man Calhoun, the family patriarch, kept clear of her if he could. When Diana, standing at the foot of the steps, shading her eyes, said, "Hello," Sue Nell just nodded.

Diana swallowed. "I came to tell you that Bo and I are in love," she said. "We want to be together, but we can't because he's afraid to tell you. So I'm telling you."

Diana waited. She swatted at a mosquito on her arm. When Sue Nell said nothing, she continued. "I've been seeing him for six months. We're in love. I think you should let him go."

Sue Nell blinked. She took a breath. She said, "You just had to come tell me."

"Bo wouldn't do it," said Diana.

"I reckon he wouldn't." Sue Nell's voice took on acidity. "You didn't stop to think *why* he wouldn't, did you? That maybe he wouldn't because he didn't want to?"

"He wants to be with me," said Diana.

"He said that?"

"Lots and lots of times."

"Why isn't he with you then?"

"He will be."

Sue Nell folded her arms. "We'll see about that."

Into the silence that lengthened between them came the sound of a motor. Bo Calhoun's Oldsmobile pulled up under the chinaberry tree in the front yard, and he stepped out of it. When he saw the women, he began to run.

He grabbed Diana's arm and shook her. "What the hell are you doing?"

"Don't be so rough," Diana began.

Sue Nell stood up. "She's been telling me you two are engaged."

"Oh my God," said Bo.

"Why not?" said Diana. "It's practically what you said. And you wouldn't tell her, and I need you now."

"Get out of here," said Bo. "Just get moving right this minute. Do you hear me?"

Diana stood rubbing her arm, her eyes wide.

"Didn't you hear me? Get along," said Bo.

Diana turned blindly and walked across the yard to her car. In a few moments, she was gone.

Bo turned to Sue Nell. "In a lot of ways, she was right," he said.

Josh Goes Fishing

Josh winced as he swallowed the bitter, lukewarm coffee and made a mental note never again to reheat the leftovers from the previous evening. It was five-thirty, he'd had only three hours' sleep, and he'd needed something. Warmed-over coffee wasn't it. He emptied the tin cup on the ground and hung it on its peg next to the camp stove. His rod and reel was propped against the shed, the bait can beside it. He picked them up and started through the woods.

A slight haze lingered under the pines. Anyone glancing at Josh would have said he was maintaining a relaxed pace, and only a careful observer would note how swiftly he made his way through the undergrowth that caught at his khaki work pants as he passed. He was walking away from the channel, maintaining a course roughly parallel with the coast.

He jumped a ditch barely deep enough to support minnows, crossed a ridge, wiped his brow, and looked around. He was at the edge of a marshy meadow of thigh-high grass divided by turgid streams. Dispersed clumps of pine and palmetto loomed against the horizon like oases in a desert. "Shoot," Josh whispered. Getting straight across would be impossible. He'd have to go around one way or the other. Moving toward the coast, the ground would get more marshy. Clutching his bait can and rod, he began dodging along the inland edge. Water seeped into his shoes and drenched his pants legs. Now, anyone who saw him would know he was in a hurry.

Jumping from clump to clump of marsh grass, half the time landing on spongy wet ground in between, Josh gradually made his way around the meadow. Past it, on high ground again at last and breathing heavily, he moved at a jog-trot through the foliage, making remarkably little noise. Not much farther on, he turned toward the ocean. The waves became more audible, and blue water sparkled through the trees. He reached the last stand of forest before dunes rolled down to an enclosed bay. Gasping, he leaned against a pine, resin fragrant and sticky against his arm.

In an inlet, floating with the calm unreality of a dream, white in the recently risen sun, were two cabin cruisers. Josh squinted, shading his eyes with his forearm. One of the boats, he knew, was Murphy's. The other. . . . He heard the roar of an engine, and the one that wasn't Murphy's began to turn toward the narrow gap in the palmettos that was the mouth of the inlet. Josh's eyes narrowed further against sun and glare. As the boat turned, he caught a jumble of letters that somehow reconstituted themselves. *Southern Star.* The boat picked up speed and, in a moment, vanished through the gap, leaving its wake to lap the shore and toss Murphy's boat like a toy in a tub.

Without hesitation, Josh turned back. This time, he gave the meadow a wider berth. The sand caked on his shoes and pants brushed off as they dried. The walk back took twice as long as the trip out.

Josh could smell coffee before he arrived at the camp. When he entered the clearing, Larry, the bristly-haired man, was stirring grits, and the blonde, Amos, was sitting on a fallen log, sipping from one of the tin mugs.

"Be damned if it ain't the fisherman," called Larry. "Should I heat up the frying pan?"

Josh made a gesture of disgust. Amos eyed him. "You catch anything?"

Josh set down the bait can and leaned his rod and reel against a tree. "They weren't biting this morning," he said. "What about a fresh cup of coffee?"

Larry brought it to him, and he sank down on the end of the log and closed his eyes.

Wesley Pays a Visit

Sun-bleached pulverized oyster shells crunched under Lily Trulock's shoes as she walked down her driveway at eight in the morning. The Trulocks' house, a weathered frame cottage with a screened porch around three sides, was set under a live oak hung with Spanish moss. Behind the house were woods. If you went far enough back in the woods you came to Brewster's Slough, a tributary of the Big Cypress River. Brewster's Slough was thickly grown with tupelo, and on its banks Lily's husband Aubrey had his apiary, a cluster of white hives in a clearing. He spent most of his days there, wearing his bee veil and puffing at the hives with his smoker, a metal instrument that resembled a watering can.

He had gone off to the apiary this morning without a word. He seemed to care about nothing but those bees. Certainly not the store. Certainly—Lily looked both ways and crossed the road—certainly not his wife.

Worrying about Aubrey was a recent and unaccustomed emotion for Lily. Having reached the age of fifty-five, she had worried about many other things—money, her daughter, Wanda, late deliveries of merchandise, fewer customers as the ferry made fewer runs. She had worried about the war in Europe, the atom bomb, the *Flying Enterprise,* Alger Hiss, the polio epidemic, and Korea. But Aubrey, until his heart attack, was just there, just Aubrey, something to be

33

taken into account the way you'd take the tides into account
before going out on the bay. As long as you followed what
you knew, there was no problem. Now, there was a problem, and Lily wasn't sure what to do.

In the mornings before she opened the store, Lily often
walked out on the ferry slip. She pretended she wanted to
check the weather, but in truth the morning didn't feel right
until she had greeted the bay and the dark line of St. Elmo.
Whether the water was gray and whitecapping under a
curtain of rain, or lazy and green and shining as it was
today, the sight gave her a feeling of satisfaction that she
was lucky enough to be standing there looking at it.

Today, however, someone else had reached the ferry slip
first. When she caught sight of the tall figure, Lily turned
away. She opened the screen door, unlocked the store, and
turned the sign from *Closed* to *Open*.

Soon, she would hear the steady engine thrumming that
meant the ferry, the *Island Queen*, was on its way. She
knew almost to the second how long the interval would be
from her first hearing the motor to its arrival at the dock.
She also could calculate approximately what she would sell
to the arriving passengers. Because summer was all but
over, there would be no suntan lotion or picnic provisions.
The people coming in would be mostly island residents on
their way to work. A couple of Milky Way bars, which she
kept in the cooler. Cigarettes. A carton of milk and a
package of doughnuts for someone who'd run for the ferry
and missed breakfast. A few soft drinks.

She got the cash drawer from the old safe in the back
room and checked through the store's dim interior to make
sure everything was tidy. The comic books were straight on
the wire rack; no bugs were caught in the glass jars that held
gumdrops and jawbreakers and sour balls, the candies
already oozing together slightly in the heat; and the nets—
made for her by Sam Perry on St. Elmo—were correctly
sorted by size.

"Praise the Lord," a voice said.

Lily sighed. Outlined against the screen door was the lanky figure of Wesley Stafford, the youth worker at the Methodist Church.

Best to be sociable. "Good morning," she said as Wesley came in. "Saw you out on the dock."

He removed a stack of folders from the Bible he carried. "Got some tracts to give the folks when the ferry comes in."

As a Methodist herself and an admirer of Paul the Evangelist, Lily had nothing against proselytizing. She was, however, beginning to find Wesley's company a bit wearing. He had been showing up to hand out tracts several times a week lately.

She took one of the folders from him and read:

> Miracles can happen in our Lives. Though your sins be as Scarlet they shall be as white as Snow. I have known in my own Life, my father made me get on my Knees and pray to Jesus when I was a Sinner. Though he slay me yet will I trust Him.
>
> There is Lust among us, and those that spread Lust among us. St. John says: *I gave her space to repent of her fornication; and she repented not. Behold, I will cast her into a bed, and them that commit adultery with her into great tribulation, except they repent of their deeds.*
>
> There is Lust among us, and those who flaunt themselves among us. And there shall be great tribulation if they do not repent.
>
> Lay your burdens on Jesus. He is the Way, the Truth, and the Light.
>
> *The Lord is my Shepherd.*

She put the leaflet on the counter. "You wrote this yourself?"

"Yes ma'am. Ran it off on the church mimeograph machine."

Lily considered. While there were no sentiments in Wesley's tract with which she would disagree, she felt that the tone wasn't as measured as she would like. She wondered if the Methodist preacher, Brother Chillingworth, was aware that Wesley was using the church mimeograph to run off essays about Lust.

"Must be about time for you to go back to seminary," she said.

Wesley clasped his big-knuckled hands. "I can do the Lord's work just as well here as at a seminary in Montgomery."

"Sounds like you think Palmetto is an evil place."

"*Go ye into all the world*, the Bible says. There are sinners here, like everywhere else."

"Shoo."

"Yes ma'am. Drinking goes on, and . . . well, I guess you'd have to say whoring, but when I say whoring I don't just mean ladies who take money and all."

Lily did not intend to sit in her own store and talk about whoring, even if it was with a seminary student. "Maybe a Christian boy shouldn't listen to that kind of gossip."

Wesley reddened. "I want to help Jesus save people."

Lily wondered if Jesus's cause suffered more because of his enemies or his helpers. She was glad to hear the first faint sounds of the *Island Queen*. "Here comes the ferry," she said, and she and Wesley walked outside to watch it.

From this far away, the *Island Queen* didn't look rusty at all but shone white in the early morning sun, cutting through the water steadily and, Lily always thought, triumphantly.

"Now, isn't that a beauty," said Wesley. Lily looked at him in surprise. There he stood with his ungainly body and his ideas about whoring and a trickle of sweat running down past the earpiece of his glasses, and he felt the same way she did about the *Island Queen*. She felt chastised.

"What you need," she said, raising her voice above the steadily louder throbbing of the engine, "is to get back to seminary so you can be a full-fledged preacher. With a church and flock and all."

Wesley shook his head. "My work is here."

He looked so stubborn and uncertain that Lily relented. "Maybe you have the calling."

They turned to watch the *Island Queen*—hulking and rusty but still, to Lily's eye, beautiful—pull into the slip. When the engine was cut off, Wesley strode forward to greet the passengers, and his "Praise the Lord" drifted back to her.

Lily turned and walked to the store, ready to turn and say good morning to her first customer.

At Sal's

Sal's Roadhouse was halfway between the Palmetto city limits and the Trulocks' store. The place had a name—Three Mile, after a stone marker beside the highway. There were other bars around Palmetto, but Sal's was the serious juke joint. If a man was with his wife, it was a good Palmetto joke to greet him with, "Have a good time at Sal's last night?" and leave him, unjustly accused, to stammer his way out of it. If a person wasn't quite himself, it was common to say, "He must've been visiting Sal." Sal's was Palmetto's synonym for a clandestine good time.

Appearances gave no clue to why Sal's had been anointed. The roadhouse was a flat-roofed building of fading, salmon-colored concrete blocks. Between it and the road was a parking lot of crushed oyster shells, and the woods—palmetto, scrub oak, pine—encroached in back. A not very bright neon champagne glass with three neon bubbles and *Sal's* written in blue script adorned the front. It was possible to miss it completely in the dark and never realize you'd passed the most notorious site in the county.

No matter the time of day, it was dark inside Sal's. The windows were painted over, and the only light came from the jukebox and a shaded bulb over the bar. Occasionally, on hot afternoons, the door was left open, admitting a beam of sunlight that caught and held the dust spinning in the air.

The door was open this afternoon. The lunch drinkers had returned to their jobs, and remaining were those who had nowhere else to go and nothing better to do. At a table in the corner, alone, drinking Southern Comfort, sat Diana Landis.

The corner table was customarily Diana's. Many things had happened at that table over the time it had been her preserve—assignations made and broken, tears, vomiting, shouting, dancing. At the moment, all was quiet. Diana, looking strained and pale, drank silently.

The bartender, a young man named Moody Winchester who had sandy hair and slightly bucked teeth, ran a damp rag over the bar and eyed Diana. A year or so ago he had spent an instructive half hour with her on the dog's blanket in the back of his uncle's pickup truck. The truck had been parked around back at the time, and Moody's cousin had taken over the bar duties so Moody could slip away.

Events had been moving swiftly toward a pleasant outcome, or at least so Moody thought, when Diana suddenly sat up and announced that she suspected the blanket had chiggers in it. She laughed at his surprise and discomfiture, and the memory of that sound made his ears feel scalded yet. By the time he persuaded her that there were no chiggers, or that if there were he'd get her some ointment for them, his possibilities for participation had deteriorated.

This had called for more mirth from Diana, and the encounter ended unhappily. Even though he had known ever since that Diana was poison, Moody still occasionally got an urge to finish what he'd started. Something told him, though, that today wouldn't be a good time.

Diana had come in an hour ago, sat down at her table, and motioned to Moody for her usual. Since then, she had moved only to convey the glass to her mouth, but she had done that regularly and was now working on her third drink. Her eyes were fixed on the flyblown photo of Rosemary

Clooney that Moody's cousin had cut out of *Photoplay* and tacked up beside the door, but Moody would have bet that Rosemary Clooney wasn't on her mind. Her glowering presence disrupted an otherwise peaceful atmosphere. The only other passion in the room was a three-way argument at the bar over what bait to use for bass.

The light from the half-opened door dimmed, and a shadow ballooned across the floor as Wesley Stafford walked in with his Bible under his arm. Moody made vigorous circling motions with his rag, glaring at the smeared bar.

Wesley extracted a piece of paper from his Bible, slid it across the bar to Moody, and said, "Praise the Lord."

"Praise the Lord," said Moody. "You want a drink?"

Wesley ignored the question. "I'm here to tell the good news." He shoved the paper closer to Moody. "The good news," he repeated.

Wesley's entrance had caught everyone's attention. Diana set her drink on the table and stared at him. He opened his Bible to a place marked with a slip of paper. *"Wine is a mocker. Strong drink is raging,"* he read in a carrying voice.

"Lord Jesus, it's the truth," said one of the drinkers.

Moody leaned across the bar and put his hand on Wesley's arm. "Excuse me, Preacher."

Wesley stopped reading. "It's the gospel. *Go ye into the world and preach—*"

"I know," said Moody, "but I don't think—"

Diana's voice cut through the room. "Hell, Moody, let the man talk."

Moody straightened. "I got nothing against him, but I don't want him bothering people."

"Then he doesn't have to talk to you. He can talk to me." She patted the chair next to her. "Come on over here, Brother Stafford." When Wesley didn't respond, she patted more insistently. "Come *on.*"

Wesley moved toward her, sat down, and placed his Bible on the table. He cut his eyes back to Moody, who was rubbing the bar and watching the two of them.

Diana leaned toward Wesley and slid a tract out of his Bible. As she unfolded it, she nodded at Moody. "Bring Brother Stafford a Southern Comfort."

Wesley's mouth set. "No."

Moody didn't move until Diana fixed him with a look. "You hear me, Moody?"

As Moody poured the drink Diana smoothed the paper out on the table and read silently. Wesley ignored the whiskey when it was set in front of him.

"I gave her space to repent of her fornication; and she repented not," Diana read aloud.

Wesley stared past her. She moved his drink closer to him. "Why don't you try a taste?" When he shook his head, she dipped her forefinger into the amber liquid, then brushed it lightly over his lower lip. Instinctively, his tongue slid out and licked at the wetness.

Diana giggled tonelessly as his face grew deeply red. "How can you preach against it if you don't know what it is?" She dipped her finger in the drink again, but this time Wesley pushed her hand away from his mouth.

She licked the finger herself. "You write nasty things about me." She tapped the paper. "Yes, I know that *is* about me. But you won't be friendly. How do you know I don't have *my* side?"

"There's only the Lord's side."

"You won't even listen to me."

Wesley leaned forward. "I'll listen."

"You aren't friendly. You won't have a drink with me." She pouted and turned away.

Wesley looked at his glass. He reached out a tentative hand toward her. "I can't," he said. "My daddy—"

Diana faced him, her lips curled. "I do all kinds of things my daddy doesn't like. You go around the county spreading trash about me, and then you won't even be nice." She watched him intently. "You won't even try," she said, her voice hoarse.

Wesley gripped the edge of the table. "I can't."

Diana sighed explosively. "Then go away."

"But I want to tell you—"

"I don't care. Go away."

"You're sending away the Word."

Diana poured the rest of her drink down her throat. "If I go to hell it'll be your fault."

Because his eyes were momentarily closed, his lips moving, he missed her quick sidelong glance. He took a breath, picked up his glass, and swallowed half the whiskey in it. His face was redder than ever. "There," he said.

Diana's mouth twitched. "Drink it all."

He emptied the glass and sat swallowing, his Adam's apple moving up and down.

Diana slid her chair closer to his. "Tell me the good news. I need some good news right now."

"Wine is a mocker." Wesley's voice was strained.

"I don't care about that. Tell me about—" She read from the tract, *"There is Lust among us, and those that spread Lust among us.* That part."

Wesley was silent.

"I know some Bible quotes," said Diana. *"Let him kiss me with the kisses of his mouth.* That's a Bible quote."

Wesley picked up his Bible. "You're making a mockery." He opened it, searched for a moment, and declaimed:

> *How much she hath glorified herself, and lived deliciously, so much torment and sorrow give her: for she saith in her heart, I sit a queen, and am no widow, and shall see no sorrow.*
>
> *Therefore shall her plagues come in one day, death, and mourning, and famine; and she shall be utterly burned with fire: for strong is the Lord God who judgeth her.*

Diana took the book and opened it to another place. *"Let him kiss me with the kisses of his mouth: for thy love is better than wine,"* she read.

Wesley snatched the Bible from her and closed it. His eyes bulged behind his glasses.

"I was just reading what it said in the Bible," said Diana. She leaned toward him and placed her hand against his chest. "I can feel your heart."

Wesley swallowed. "I want to bring you to Jesus."

"You like me that much?"

"Jesus loves you."

"No. I mean *you*. I'm tired of men who act sweet at first and then treat me hateful. You like me?"

Wesley hesitated, then nodded.

Diana stood. She trailed her fingers along his chest and brought them to rest against the side of his neck. "Then let's go."

Wesley stood slowly and tucked his Bible under his arm. He followed Diana out the door. Moody Winchester stopped polishing the bar to watch them go.

On the Boat

The boat's tiny cabin was stifling. Diana barely glanced at the bunk with its rumpled sheets. She took a bottle of Southern Comfort and two glasses from a cabinet and put them on the counter next to a fishing reel.

"No," said Wesley. He steadied himself against the door frame.

Diana poured a drink and swallowed it.

"You have to stop these ways," said Wesley. "If you don't you'll go to hell."

"I'm there now," said Diana.

She crossed the cabin and stood in front of him. "You really need those glasses?" In a quick gesture, she stood on tiptoe and took them from his face, then stepped back out of his reach.

Wesley shook his head in surprise, his face naked without the heavy black frames, his eyes small and pink-rimmed. "You give those back."

Diana put them on. "Ooh," she said. "Everything's all blurry."

Wesley lunged forward. "Give them to me."

Diana sidestepped, giggling. "I want to see how I look." She stood in front of one of the windows, trying to get a reflection. "I can't even *see*. They're making me go cross-eyed."

"Stop it, now." Wesley's voice was anxious.

"Stop what?"

"Give me my glasses."

She walked to the bunk. "Come get them." She took them off and held them out.

He walked toward her and put out his hand. She put the glasses behind her back. "I changed my mind. I want them some more."

"No!"

She put them on again. "They make me so *dizzy*," she said, and collapsed on the bunk.

Wesley fell on top of her, grabbing at her shoulders as she started to squirm away. She made feeble efforts at escape and then they lay still, panting. "Well now," Diana said.

"Give them to me."

Diana took off the glasses and put them on the floor beside the bunk. "You won't be needing them for a little bit." She slid her arms around his waist and pulled him closer. "Will you?"

Wesley made a strangled sound as Diana pressed against him. "No," she said softly, "I can tell you won't be needing those for the next while."

Wesley strained her to him and covered her face with wet, feverish kisses. "You," he said. "You're nothing but a whore."

"Just like the whore of Babylon."

He burrowed against her, breathing hard. "You flaunt yourself—" A thump interrupted him. They looked down to see his Bible, which had fallen from the bunk to the floor, the tracts scattered around it. "Forgive me, Jesus," Wesley said.

"It's all right." Diana reached out to him, but he flung her hand away. He put on his glasses and began to gather the tracts.

"For heaven's sake." Diana sat up and touched his shoulder.

"Stop that, you harlot." Wesley stood up and backed away from her. "You have to stop this. You have to repent." He glanced wildly around the cabin, and his eye fell on the fishing reel. He picked it up. "You have to stop this."

Diana eyed him warily and started to get up as he approached, but he caught her and pinned her arms behind her back. "Let me go," she said.

"You have to stop." He wound the heavy-duty line around and around her wrists.

"Don't do that. It hurts."

He cut the line with his pocket knife and tied it off. Then he began winding it around her ankles. "Don't do that! Let me go!"

"I want you to think," said Wesley. "I don't want you to move and flaunt yourself. I want you to think and pray to Jesus."

"You're crazy."

She was sitting on the edge of the bunk, ankles and wrists tied. Her voice took on a wheedling tone. "Let me go, all right? I'll go to church with you. I'll pray to Jesus. We'll get right down on our knees and pray together. I repent. I promise."

Wesley looked doubtful, then shook his head. "You've got to think and pray alone first. Like Jesus in the garden. I'll come back in an hour, and we'll pray together then."

Tears welled up in Diana's eyes. "Don't leave me tied up like this. Please."

"Take your troubles to Jesus." Wesley made a gesture of benediction, tucked his Bible under his arm, and was gone.

Josh and the Southern Star

Josh, at the tiller of his boat, surveyed the coast of the mainland as it caught the late afternoon sun. The creeks, inlets, and hidden bays could provide hundreds of places for a cabin cruiser like the *Southern Star* to hide. Besides, the boat could have traveled miles since he saw it rendezvous with Murphy this morning. The probable futility of his mission was as oppressive as the heat.

It had been difficult to get away from the island. "You got your pay, boy," Murphy had sneered. "Can't you wait a few days to spend it?" Josh had persisted because this was his only chance. Tomorrow they made another run. Murphy had at last grudgingly consented to let him go. "You sure do like to june around," he said, squinting at Josh. "They must train you to be june bugs up there at Columbus."

"I reckon."

"You don't get no more money till next month, so don't go spend all this and come asking."

"Naw, I won't."

Still, Murphy hesitated, asking Josh delaying questions. Had he stirred the mash? Checked the cooker for tomorrow, made sure the kerosene blowers were working? When Josh's answers were satisfactory, Murphy thought of several meaningless chores for Josh to do before, with evident reluctance, he said, "Go on, but I want you back here before dark. You understand?" Outwardly obliging, Josh nearly ripped his starter cord to pieces getting the motor cranked.

He followed the coast. Here were lagoons and bays where brownish green grass, waist high, extended into the water and hummocky islands supported a few spikes of palmetto or silver-trunked, moss-hung, leafless trees, long since strangled by the salt water. Occasionally an egret, standing long-legged, motionless, and white against the grass and water, became shy at the sound of his motor and flapped away.

The sun slanted lower. Soon, he would reach the Palmetto city limits. The last landmark before that was the mouth of the canal that connected the Big Cypress River and the bay. Maybe he should turn back, Josh thought as he reached the canal and its rearing steel drawbridge. Then he remembered seeing boats berthed in a makeshift marina half a mile or so up the estuary. He turned beneath the bridge up the dark brown canal.

The canal was wide, lined to the water's edge on either side with trees trailing Spanish moss. After a few minutes Josh saw ahead a rickety complex of docks at which half a dozen boats were moored. Overlooking it in a clearing on the bank was a shack with a sign *Live Bait* nailed to the front door.

He recognized the *Southern Star* before he saw the name. Somehow, in the glimpse he'd gotten as the boat had swung away from Murphy's, he'd taken in the narrow blue stripe around the hull, the flash of blue-and-white curtains at the windows. Pretty fancy boat, Josh thought. Curtains and all. He rode past just to be sure, but he knew he could've picked it from among fifty. He cut his motor and drifted in.

The landing, as far as he could tell, was deserted. There were no boat owners working on their crafts or sitting out with a beer in the fading light. Josh checked the *Live Bait* hut. The door was fastened with a rusty padlock. Then he walked down the dock to the *Southern Star*.

His tentative call of greeting brought no response, so he

jumped to the deck. Glancing around, he walked swiftly to the steps down to the entrance of the cabin. The door stood open.

The light inside was dim, filtered through the curtains. He slid them back and looked around. On one side of the enclosure was a counter with fishing gear and a bottle of Southern Comfort and two glasses on it. On the other was a bunk, its rumpled sheets trailing. A fishing reel had unwound, its line making a wavy pattern across the floor. It trailed through a spray of dark spots.

The wheel was forward. He checked the chart compartment and found a map of *Palmetto–St. Elmo Sound,* but no indication of who the boat's owner might be.

He returned below and began to search in earnest. The red ice chest contained nothing but a half inch of water in the bottom. The cupboard beneath the sink yielded three cokes. The kitchen drawer harbored various implements of cutlery and a pack of Luckies. He cursed under his breath and wiped the sweat from his eyes.

He had started to cross the cabin to check the storage area beneath the bunk, when his foot slipped. Cursing again, he looked down and saw that the spray of dark spots on the floor was now a long smear. He bent, touched it, and rubbed the fluid between his fingers.

The back of his neck went suddenly stiff. He wiped his hand on his shirt pocket and looked around. Then he headed for the door.

He was standing on the edge of the dock when he saw something floating. It was submerged a few feet below the surface of the murky water, yet suspended, twisting with the vagaries of the current. Josh knelt. It was a blurred white figure. The figure, he saw, was entwined in a net—a cast net with its circumference lined with lead weights to make it sink. One side of the net had caught in a crack where the wood of the piling holding the dock had split, and it hadn't sunk.

Josh's mouth filled with fluid. He choked it down and

looked again. The figure caught in the net was not, as he had been trying to tell himself, a large fish or a sodden pile of cloth. Dark hair swam around what was unmistakably a woman's head. A hand floated free. At any moment, a boat might come by. Its wake would wash her loose.

As he watched, the dark shape of a catfish swam up and nuzzled at her fingers. Josh's body shuddered repeatedly, but, unwilling to leave a trace of his presence, he managed not to vomit.

After a few minutes, he got weakly to his feet, drenched with sweat. What he had to do, and do right now, was get away.

A Telephone Call

The throb of the *Island Queen's* engine was fading, and inside Trulock's Grocery & Marine Supply the only other sound was of Lily's broom scratching the wooden floor. She had turned off the fan so it wouldn't blow the dust, and heat had crept slowly into the room.

Overall, it had been a pretty good day. The after-school candy business had picked up again now that the fall session had started. That almost, but not quite, made up for the exodus of summer people who rented cottages on St. Elmo or the beach. This year she must have sold nearly a dozen red tin pail-and-shovel sets over the summer, half of them to perspiring parents whose wailing child had just remembered his own set, back home in Atlanta.

She hadn't sold any pails and shovels today, but what with candy, cold drinks, cotton thread for net-mending, and lead for weights, she had done well enough. Not to mention popsicles, which were always popular when it got as hot as this. She could use more of the lime-flavored ones.

Once again, Aubrey hadn't shown up for lunch. What he ate down there in the swamp she couldn't imagine, unless it was honeycomb. Before his attack, he had done half the work at the store; now he did practically nothing. Of course he was—she counted mentally—sixty-three, but that wasn't old enough to act like you were already dead. That heart attack might as well have killed him, she thought, shocking herself.

She swept the dust out the screen door and gave the concrete steps a quick going-over. Then she straightened the comics that drooped, dog-eared, in the round wire rack: *Archie, Little Lulu,* the classic of *The Hunchback of Notre Dame*. Lily leafed through a *True Love*. The girls from the high school hung around drinking cokes and reading those for hours, poring over the heroes with patent-leather hair, the busty, big-eyed, tearful heroines, the kisses at the end, lovers silhouetted against a yellow moon. It wasn't up to Lily, thank goodness, to tell the high school girls what it all amounted to.

Those bees. Aubrey had always kept a few hives. It brought in extra money, but . . . She looked at the glass jars of golden liquid on their special shelf, with the sign she had lettered saying *Our Own Honey*. *Our* honey! That was back when she'd been happy that Aubrey was interested in something again. While he was off taking care of *our* honey, somebody had to look after their livelihood, and it looked like she had been nominated. She went to the back room to put the broom away.

She was vaguely conscious of hearing an outboard motor, then hearing it stop, and she thought in passing that whoever it was should be getting home, because it was almost dark. She hoped it wasn't motor trouble. When somebody's motor cut out nearby, she often had to drive him all the way to Palmetto.

She moved back into the store, and at the same time heard running feet pounding on the boardwalk that led from the ferry slip. The sounds stopped for a moment or two, and Lily heard harsh breathing. A moment later, a young man rushed in, slamming the screen door behind him, and stood in front of the counter, chest heaving.

He looked about twenty-five, Lily thought, and he was dressed like a workman in filthy, stained khaki pants and a short-sleeved shirt wet with sweat. Had he been less dirty, he would have been nice-looking—deeply tanned, black curls, dark eyes. He looked like he had something important on his mind.

"Help you?" she offered, wondering what was the matter with him.

Having run so desperately to get there, he seemed to have forgotten why. He looked at her blankly, perspiration running into his eyebrows.

"I said . . ." Lily began, pitching her voice a bit louder, and at that he focused his eyes.

"Change," he said.

"What?"

He shook his head and dug into his pants pocket. He held out a limp dollar bill. "Nickel for the phone," he said.

Lily chuckled. "*I* see what you want." She glanced at the cash register. "Wouldn't you know I already locked up the cash drawer."

Although the young man didn't say anything or move, simply continued to stand holding out his dollar, Lily sensed that what she had said wasn't what he wanted to hear. He obviously would not yield to refusal. "Just hang on a second and I'll get it for you," she said.

The safe, which Aubrey had insisted they buy years ago, was in the back room. Lily hurried to it, at the same time calling back to him, "Can't imagine how it got this hot. 'Course, I say that every year, I reckon. Wonder if it means there'll be a hurricane. It's better to have this than snow, though, from all I hear, not that I ever saw snow." She pulled at the ribbon around her neck that held the key to the safe. "You ever see snow? I mean, falling down?"

At first, it seemed as if he wouldn't answer, then she heard a strangled, "No'm."

"Me neither." She fitted the key into the lock. "Wouldn't mind seeing it one day, though." The safe swung open, and from the cash drawer inside she took three quarters, two dimes, and a nickel. When she turned, she saw that he'd followed her, still proffering the dollar. "This what you need?"

He shoved the dollar at her and all but snatched the change out of her hand. Before she could blink, the screen had banged behind him. A moment later, she heard the door of the phone booth bang as well.

She felt cheated. Smoothing the dollar, relocking the safe, she wondered what on earth the rush was. Other people didn't mind visiting for a few minutes, especially if Lily was doing them a favor by getting them change. There weren't so many people out here at the beach, after all, that they could afford to be standoffish with one another. She heard running again and watched as the young man headed for the dock through the dusk. After all that, his phone call hadn't lasted even two minutes.

Without stopping to think about it, she slipped through the screen door. His motor sputtered and caught, and she saw him turn his boat toward St. Elmo. She watched him cross the water. He headed for the south end of the island, and she wondered briefly if he knew where he was going. There were no houses down that way. None of her business, after all, and if he *did* get lost that was none of her business either.

She went back to the store, locked it, and then, as she always did, walked along the beach for a few minutes. Removing her sandals, dangling them by the straps, she let the cooling waves slide around her ankles. As the swells spilled onto the shore, she could see a flicker of phosphorus in the water. The white sand was almost luminous in the dying rays of the sun. Lily stood still, thinking of nothing. A muscle twitched in her neck, then subsided. She turned back to see if Aubrey had come home for supper.

The Fish Fry

That evening, as Josh was hurrying back to St. Elmo, the Palmetto Kiwanis Club's Candidates' Night Fish Fry was getting under way in the city park. Long trestle tables under the pines were draped with heavy white paper. The roofless enclosure where cooking was done over camp stoves by sweating Kiwanians was surrounded by smoke and the smell of grease.

At a Kiwanis fish fry, everyone who paid a dollar got deep-fried mullet, grits, hush puppies, slaw, coffee or iced tea. By six o'clock, the line of people fanning themselves with paper plates snaked to the edge of the park. The Palmetto mosquito-control truck had driven through the area a couple of hours before emitting an all but impenetrable fog of DDT, so the insects weren't biting too badly.

At a right angle to the tables stood a makeshift bandstand on which Sonny Smith and his Bluegrass Boys were playing dinner music, including their version of "Sleepin' at the Foot of the Bed," a local favorite. Red, white, and blue crepe-paper streamers hung limply at the corners of the bandstand. Also on the bandstand, behind Sonny and his boys, were rows of folding chairs for the candidates. None of the chairs was occupied, since the candidates were mixing with the crowd and handing out cards with their names and slogans printed on them.

The slogan on Snapper Landis's card was, *A Decade of Experience;* Gospel Roy McInnes's said, *A Family Man of Integrity.* Standing under a pine tree, a circle of men around him, Snapper was telling how he had headed off Gospel Roy's efforts to get an extra spot on the program by offering to sing "The Old Rugged Cross" as the invocation.

"I told them," said Snapper, glancing around to make sure he had everyone's attention, "I told them if Roy sang 'The Old Rugged Cross' they had to let *me* sing 'Good Night, Irene.' They moved on quick to the next order of business."

Roy was helping the Kiwanians' wives put ice in paper cups and pour tea. His obvious sincerity and virtue, coupled with his wavy hair and booming baritone voice, had made half the ladies in the First Baptist choir fall in love with him. They brought pound cakes and loaves of Sally Lunn to choir practice for him, and last Christmas they chipped in and bought him a new rod and reel. "All I'm saying is, we need a man in the job you good people can be *proud* of," Gospel Roy was saying, and the Kiwanians' wives nodded and thought they could surely be proud of Gospel Roy.

When everybody was served, Sonny Smith finished his program with a bluegrass version of "Dixie," and he and his boys retired from the stage. After an invocation by Brother Chillingworth, the Methodist preacher, and the pledge of allegiance, the candidates—for city and county commission, for school board, for supervisor of elections—began having their say. Snapper sat in his folding chair, apparently rapt at the rhetoric. Gospel Roy adopted an attitude reminiscent of prayer, leaning forward with his hands clasped between his knees.

The speakers droned on, cigarettes were ground out in paper plates, and children began to whine. Lights that had been strung in the trees' lower branches were turned on, attracting whatever insects were still alive. When the fourth

candidate for county commission reiterated his final promise, it was time for the candidates for the state house of
representatives to take the platform.

Because he was the incumbent, and also because the
president of the Kiwanis was a buddy of his, Snapper had
been allowed to speak last. Gospel Roy got up, straightened
his tie, and began with, "My Friends. . . ."

Before Roy was well into his introductory jokes, Sheriff
Woody Malone and Cecil Banks, his deputy, appeared at
the edge of the crowd. Their presence was not unusual, as
any public function called for at least a brief appearance to
show everyone that Woody was on the job. Tonight,
though, there was a noticeable pallor on Woody's usually
ruddy face, and Cecil, a fastidious young man who changed
his clothes several times a day in hot weather, was smeared
with mud and his pants legs were wet to the knee.

After a short but intense conversation with Woody, Cecil
threaded his way through the tables to the bandstand and
plucked at Snapper's sleeve. Heads turned and weight
shifted among the audience as Cecil and Snapper entered
into a whispered conversation that was, no question about
it, rude to Gospel Roy, who was trying to make his speech.

Gospel Roy became distracted and annoyed. "If my
opponent would do me the courtesy to listen, in case he has
to answer to these charges . . ." he said, glancing over at
Snapper, who was shaking his head at Cecil.

Now, the crowd was paying more attention to Cecil and
Snapper than to Gospel Roy. Heads turned to one another
in inquiry, and people craned their necks toward Woody,
who was standing in the back, fingering his holster.

Gospel Roy carried on gamely in the face of this mass
distraction, but nobody at all was listening to him by the
time Snapper cried, "Great God Almighty!" and jumped to
his feet, his folding chair clanging over behind him.

He jumped from the bandstand and followed Cecil
through the crowd, half-running. When they reached

Woody, the three turned and headed through the trees, and in a moment a County Sheriff's Department car flashed by.

Back on the bandstand, Gospel Roy was fumbling. "I don't know why my honored opponent has felt it necessary—" he began, when he was interrupted by Fish Arnold, the challenger for the post of supervisor of elections. Fish, a colorless individual whom nobody could imagine running for office, had been sitting next to Snapper. He got up and, with a polite nod to Gospel Roy, commandeered the microphone. "Ladies and gentlemen," he said, "I regret to tell you Congressman Landis has had to leave. From what I overheard Deputy Barnes saying, his daughter Diana has been murdered."

The hullabaloo that followed consisted of shouted questions and general milling about and conjecture. Fish Arnold was the central figure until it became evident that he had told exactly as much as he knew and no amount of pumping would produce further information. He then faded into the background.

Afterward, however, when Palmetto's soothsayers totaled up profits and losses, they decided that two people were sure election winners as a result of Candidates' Night. One was Fish Arnold; the other was Snapper Landis.

Family Meeting

Four late-model Oldsmobiles were pulled up under a live oak tree in the front yard of the rambling house. Any Palmetto resident who drove by the place, five miles or so out of town, could have made an educated guess about what was going on. "Old Man Calhoun's got the boys out to his place," the person might say. "Reckon they're about ready to get the new still set up."

In fact, the Calhouns were working steadily on their new moonshine operation. They had a location in the river swamp, with a ditch excavated and a log frame built around it. Construction was proceeding on schedule, but the new still was not the reason Old Man Calhoun had summoned Bo, Sonny, Lester, and Purvis to their childhood home. Old Man Calhoun had other things on his mind.

The living room at the Calhouns', where the old man was reading the riot act to his sons, showed evidence of a fundamental difference of outlook between the old man, who had spent most of his life in the swamp making moonshine, and his wife, Miss Myrna, who was a member of the Daughters of the American Confederacy and had pretensions to culture. Gold-framed reproductions of *Pinky* and *The Blue Boy* hung on one wall; a businesslike rack of shotguns on the other. Most of the furniture was a version of French provincial designed by someone who had never

been north of Macon, but the chair in which the old man sat
was worn, nondescript, and obviously just right for his
scrawny behind. China quail billed on the coffee table,
while beneath it Deacon, the old man's fourteen-year-old
bird dog, scratched and broke wind.

Dominating the room was a console-model television set,
the first ever in Palmetto when the four Calhoun boys had
given it to their parents two years ago. Since the nearest
broadcasting station was a hundred miles away in Tallahassee, the set rarely picked up anything but snow despite the
tallest antenna money could buy. This didn't prevent the
Calhouns from having it turned on all day long and, the
sound a bare murmur, it was on now.

The old man's voice was bumpy with phlegm, and spittle
gathered at the corners of his mouth as he spoke. The boys
sprawled on the uncomfortable furniture, all looking as if
they were listening to something they had heard before.

Purvis, the baby at age twenty-six, finally interrupted.
"Daddy," he said, speaking loudly and slowly, "we've said
if we find out who done it they'll be sorry. But what else can
we do?"

Old Man Calhoun's sparse gray hair stuck out featherlike
from the top of his head. He blinked at Purvis, looking like
a baby bird. "I don't give a good goddamn—" he began, but
Bo waved his hand, saying in a low voice, "Don't bother
him about it, Purv."

Bo, the second son, was the unofficial leader of the
younger Calhouns. Sonny, the eldest, was too soft, Lester
too dumb, and Purvis too young for the position. Bo was the
only one the old man would shut up for. Although the room
fell silent, Bo seemed disinclined to continue. He was, in
fact, more distracted than he usually was at Calhoun family
meetings.

Before the old man got his breath back, Bo's wife Sue
Nell entered the room and said, "Miss Myrna wants to
know do you-all want coffee."

Sue Nell was more than any of the Calhouns, including the old man, could handle. Quirky and given to sulks, she had alienated the more conventional wives of the other Calhoun sons, who retaliated by telling each other she was cruel to her three children, although there was no evidence of this. She and Miss Myrna got along only marginally, Sue Nell pretending no interest in the Daughters of the American Confederacy. Her offer of coffee was an uncommon occurrence. She looked bad today, her skin the color of curdled milk.

"I'll drink a cup, sugar," said the old man, and Sonny, Lester, and Purvis nodded assent. She looked at Bo. "Do you want some, William?"

"Sure, honey," he said, not looking at her.

When she left the room, Lester said, "How come it is she called you William?"

Bo shrugged. "It's my name."

"Yes, but—" Lester began, but Old Man Calhoun evidently felt he had yielded the floor long enough.

"What I say," he began, "is that nobody blows up a Calhoun's still and gets away with it. Don't you boys have a bit of pride? If my daddy had saw that, he would've pumped every ass in the county full of buckshot. But you boys—you boys let the time go by, and—"

Sue Nell reentered, carrying mugs on a tray. "Help yourself, *William*," snickered Lester in an undertone. Sue Nell glanced at him, her eyes poisonous. The mugs rattled when she set the tray on the coffee table, startling Deacon and sending him, toenails clicking, down the hall. Somewhere in the house a phone rang once.

"Daddy," Bo said distinctly, "I will promise you this. We'll get even. Take my word that we're working on it. Will you do that for me?"

"I be goddamn . . ." started the old man, but subsided when Sue Nell handed him his coffee.

He slurped at it, attention distracted. Sue Nell sat on the

arm of a chair while the Calhoun sons talked among themselves.

"I been in touch with Elmore," said Sonny.

"What'd he say?" asked Purvis.

"Well. . . ." Sonny put sugar and cream in his coffee. "He didn't say a whole lot, but looks to me like he ain't hurting while we're out of business. He *says* he's cutting back, but I tell you the truth. I think he's getting liquor somewhere else."

Lester socked his fist into his palm. "I'd sure like to get ahold of that—"

"Shut up." Bo glanced at their father, who was drinking noisily, then surveyed his brothers. "You all know what we have to do?"

"Watch Elmore," Sonny said.

"Damn right, watch him," said Bo. "Find out who the hell he's getting that whiskey from. Find out, and you'll find the son of a bitch that blew up the still."

The room was silent except for the old man's slobbering. Then came the sound of footsteps, and Miss Myrna entered the room.

Miss Myrna, small and white-haired, had spent her life turning her back on what her husband did for a living. The effort had left her dazed, and befuddlement was her usual expression. Now, however, she looked more alert than usual. "The most awful thing," she said. She looked around, waiting until the old man noticed her and put his coffee cup down.

"That was Voncile, down at the post office," she said. "There's been a murder. At the landing." She stopped to let attention build. "Diana Landis got beat to death with a cast net and thrown in the water. She was hanging there all tangled up."

A second or two of shocked silence followed. Bo, with a convulsive motion of his arm, knocked his mug of coffee to the floor. Sue Nell stared at him, her eyes brackish in her pale face.

Miss Myrna looked at the spilled coffee and said, "Oh my."

"What happened? Somebody killed?" snapped Old Man Calhoun.

Miss Myrna leaned closer to him. "Diana Landis!" she bawled. "Snapper's daughter! Murdered!"

"I swan," said the old man.

Miss Myrna did her best to answer the questions that followed, but she knew little else except that Sheriff Malone had discovered the body after getting an anonymous phone call telling him where to look.

"Do they know who did it?" Bo's voice sounded pinched.

"No idea at all, Voncile said."

"One of her gentlemen friends, most likely," said Sue Nell. Her lips were trembling.

"She's dead and gone now," said Miss Myrna. "Don't speak ill."

Bo and Sue Nell looked at each other. Sue Nell seemed about to speak, then pursed her lips. Bo's face, pale up till then, began to grow pink.

Miss Myrna cleared her throat. "How about if I get you all some cake?"

Bo didn't seem to hear her. He got up and walked out the front door. In a moment, the Calhouns heard the sound of his car engine, which soon faded as he drove away.

Condolence Call

Lily took the peach cobbler out of the oven, turned off the gas, and swayed, overcome by the heat. Jell-O mold would have been easier and cooler, but on these occasions it was important to take trouble. Setting the hot dish down and removing her apron, she walked out of the kitchen and sank into the rocking chair on the screened porch, leaning back and pulling the damp, humid air into her lungs. She'd have to bathe before she left.

Sitting in tepid, rust-colored water in the deep, claw-footed tub, dusting herself with talcum powder afterward, Lily wondered how Snapper really felt about Diana's death. He was sure to do and say the proper things, but it was no secret that Diana's reputation had hurt him in the last election, and the challenge from Gospel Roy was the strongest he'd ever had. "Talks about weeding out the subversives. He can't even handle his own daughter"—Lily had heard that more than once since the campaign had gotten under way.

Still—she pulled her second-best dress, navy with white polka dots, over her head—a daughter was a daughter. Lily didn't always see eye-to-eye with her own daughter, Wanda. Wanda, Lily had always thought, lacked spunk. Marrying Woody Malone was a good example. But Lily certainly would be terribly upset if Wanda were murdered, spunk or no spunk.

It was too bad Diana's mother had died, and Snapper had

always been so busy. The girl had been left to the maid, Pearl, who did her best, but. . . . Lily zipped her dress and ran a comb through her hair.

The cobbler had cooled a bit. Lily stuck the adhesive tape on which she had printed *Trulock* to the bottom of the dish, pulled on her white gloves, and, carrying the cobbler and with her white purse under her arm, she started out.

Once she had the Trulocks' Nash pointed toward the highway, she resisted the temptation to detour by the store and see how the Eubanks girl, who'd agreed to see to the place for the afternoon, was getting along. There really wasn't time, and, besides, Sara Eubanks got sulky if she thought you didn't trust her.

When Lily pulled up at Snapper's house, the circular drive in front was already filled with cars. She parked on the shoulder of the road and made her way to the front door, which stood half-open, a babble of voices drifting out. She pressed the bell, and in a moment a tall black woman, hook-nosed and broad-shouldered, appeared. Lily recognized Marinda Washington, daughter of Snapper's maid, Pearl.

"Evening, Marinda," said Lily. "Came to pay respects to Snapper."

"Yes'm." Marinda opened the door wider, and Lily stepped inside.

The smell of coffee drifted from the dining room on her left, while across the entry hall the living room was full of voices and smoke. "Lot of people here already?"

"A right smart of 'em," said Marinda.

"Peach cobbler," said Lily, offering Marinda the dish.

Marinda received it without comment, and Lily thought how much less pleasant she was than her mother. "Where's Pearl?" she asked.

"Not here." Marinda turned and started down the hallway toward the kitchen, tossing "coffee and cake in the dining room" over her shoulder.

The dining room was set with cut-glass plates of sliced

pound cake, banana nut bread, and Lane cake. The silver
coffee service, presided over by the ladies of the Wesleyan
Service Guild, was on the sideboard. An assortment of
townsfolk was gathered around the table, talking and chewing, the crumbs trickling into Snapper's floral-patterned
carpet.

Lily got coffee and pound cake and crossed the hall into
the living room. Snapper was there, surrounded by six or
seven solemn-faced Palmetto citizens. He wore a black
suit, stiff white shirt, and black tie, and was nodding to a
group of departing guests.

"Blessed be the name of the Lord," he said as Lily
walked up. He turned to her, seized her hand, and said,
"Miz Trulock."

"I'm sorry to hear about Diana," Lily said, feeling
slightly awkward. "I remember when she used to buy candy
from me."

Snapper's eyes glistened. "The Lord giveth and the Lord
taketh away," he said.

Someone brought her a chair and she joined the group
around Snapper. Turning to Brother Chillingworth, whose
bald head glistened in the close atmosphere, Snapper said,
"Woody wasn't there when the call came in. Cecil took it
and he thought it was a joke."

Lily felt uncomfortable at the mention of her son-in-law
and his deputy. Woody, as she saw it, was little more than a
laughingstock.

"Cecil was still chuckling over it when Woody got there,"
Snapper went on, "and since he didn't believe it was
serious he can't remember a teetotaling thing the man said.
He thinks it was just, 'There's a body hanging in a net under
the docks on the canal.' But you know how Cecil is."

"Got no business being a deputy," said a disgruntled
listener.

Snapper made a pacific gesture. "I don't say that. The
law enforcement in this county is the finest of anywhere. I

completely trust Woody and Cecil to find out who killed my little girl."

How strange it is, thought Lily, that Diana's death has peeled ten or twelve years from her age. Instead of the twenty-year-old troublemaker she was, who had gone to bed with—Lily glanced around—three or four men in this room, she had become in memory the motherless child whose passing was easier to regret.

"But who the hell—excuse me" (the last was for Lily's benefit) "would call up like that and leave no name?" one of the group wanted to know.

"The one that did it, that's who," retorted another.

Snapper shook his head. "Let Woody and Cecil figure it out. They're the experts."

Lily doubted Woody was an expert in anything except grunting for earthworms on the courthouse lawn. Something else was bothering her, though. "You mean they found out about the murder because of this telephone call?" she asked.

"Yes ma'am," said Snapper. "Cecil took it, like I said, but when Woody came in after his supper he thought maybe they should see about it. They took a run out there, and. . . ." He bent his head and reached for his handkerchief.

"Hold on, boy," someone said.

Snapper mopped his face. "Lordy," he said.

"What time did the call come in?" asked Lily.

Snapper shrugged. "Six or so, I reckon."

Brother Chillingworth gripped Lily's shoulder and whispered, "Don't make him talk about it." Lily lapsed into silence, but not because of Brother Chillingworth. A picture had come into her memory. A young man, black curly hair, dark eyes, holding out a wrinkled dollar bill. At six o'clock, or thereabouts.

"Where's your old man?" Snapper had to repeat his question before Lily realized it was addressed to her.

"Aubrey? Oh . . . he wasn't feeling well enough to come. He said to give you his condolences." Only after the sentence was out did Lily realize she hadn't thought twice about the lie. Aubrey, at his apiary since dawn, didn't even know about Diana.

Lily rose. "I'll be going."

Snapper stood and took her hand. "Thank you for coming, Miss Lily. You can tell that old man of yours I said to take care of himself."

She picked her way through the crowd and let herself out the front door. When she got the Nash started, she didn't turn toward the beach and the store. Instead, she swung the car toward town, the courthouse, and the office of Sheriff Woody Malone.

Bo and Sue Nell

"She made a humming noise in the back of her throat," said Bo Calhoun.

It was late afternoon, the same hour Lily was sipping coffee at Snapper's house. Bo was drunk. He was sitting on the front steps of his house, a jar of pale liquid and a glass at his feet. The air was heavy, sweet with honeysuckle that overhung the porch and made, where the sun shone through it, dappled patterns on Sue Nell's yellow blouse.

She stood behind him, taut, near the front door. At her feet was a worn duffel bag. She was going, she told Bo, to stay at the Calhouns' fish camp on Tupelo Branch. The only access to the camp was by boat. When she told him she was going, Bo said only, "Take your boat this time. That's what I bought that damn bateau for. I'm sick of you going off in mine." The house was empty, the children sent to visit their cousins at Uncle Sonny's. On the floor inside, glittering where the light picked them out, were shards of crystal goblets that had belonged to Bo's mother's mother, goblets that had been carefully portioned out to Miss Myrna's sons as each married. When Sue Nell had smashed the last one on the wall next to the chair where he was sitting and drinking, Bo had picked up his jar and glass and stumbled out. He had only gotten across the porch to the steps before he had to sit down. "A humming," he repeated.

"What else?" Sue Nell's voice was harsh. Bo didn't reply. She strode down the steps and turned to face him. When he refused to meet her eyes, she slapped his face, the solid sound of the blow attesting to the strength behind it.

Bo swayed to one side slightly, his head still bent. When he regained his balance, he said, "She would say things. Call out."

"Call what?"

"Call me, I guess I mean."

"When you were doing it? When she got her feelings?"

Bo closed his eyes.

Sue Nell leaned close to him. Almost whispering, she said, "She must have told you how you were better than anybody else. Did she say that?" She jerked his chin up, forcing him to look at her. "Answer me."

"Yes."

She let go of his face with a choked laugh. "You ought to be proud, Bo. The very best in all of Palmetto. She had a lot to go by for comparison."

For the first time, Bo was roused from passivity. He looked up at Sue Nell. "She wasn't doing that anymore," he said. "Not since me."

She twisted off a tendril of honeysuckle and began stripping it of its leaves. Bo tipped the contents of his glass down his throat.

"She wrote poems," he said. "Rhymes."

Sue Nell didn't reply, but he seemed almost eager to continue. "She would read them to me. She could always make it come out so it rhymed."

"Poems," Sue Nell said. Her voice had lost its edge.

"Songs, like," said Bo. "Only without a tune."

Sue Nell sat down on the step below Bo's and rested her head on her knees. Bo, staring ahead, didn't look at her. "She'd bring me a new one every so often," he said. "She liked to write them. She'd say—"

"Hush," said Sue Nell.

Bo stopped, confused. "But you were asking, making me tell you everything, all about what we did—"

"Just hush."

Bo tipped several inches of liquid into his glass and swallowed half of it. He waved the glass at Sue Nell. "Want a drink?"

She rocked her head back and forth against her knees. When she spoke, her voice was rough. "Why did you do it, Bo?"

He rolled the glass between his hands. "I don't know."

"Were you in love with her?"

"She gave me a lot of trouble."

"Yes, but—"

"She's dead now, it doesn't matter."

"Yes, she's dead. She's dead." Sue Nell raised her head and turned her wet face toward her husband.

Lily at the Courthouse

The county courthouse was a two-story building of dusty-red brick, topped by a clock tower and overlooking a lawn of tired-looking grass. It stood on the corner of the beach highway and Milton Avenue, a heat-baked street with a straggling line of drugstore, dime store, hardware store, grocery store, and filling station.

Parking the Nash in front, Lily glanced across the street to Maude's Coffee Cup, where she suspected Woody spent much of his time. He wasn't there. With Diana Landis's body on his hands, he must've decided to do some work.

On the courthouse door was a sign with Snapper's picture and the slogan, *Reelect Robert "Snapper" Landis, Your Congressman*. Lily walked past it into the dim interior with its hardwood floors, droning hall fans, and dull green walls.

The Sheriff's Department was a left turn off the main hall. Entering the pebble-glass door, Lily saw immediately that activity had replaced the former sleepy atmosphere of the office. Loyce, Woody's secretary, wasn't cutting recipes out of the *Woman's Home Companion* but was banging away at her typewriter, her jaws flailing at a wad of gum, the light flashing off her harlequin glasses.

The door of Woody's office, behind Loyce, was closed, a circumstance unique in Lily's memory. As Lily walked in, Deputy Cecil Barnes emerged from it to rush over and put a sheet of paper on Loyce's desk. Cecil nodded at Lily, said,

"Ma'am," and returned to Woody's office, closing the door behind him. Loyce glanced up briefly but didn't stop typing.

After waiting several seconds, Lily said, "Don't mean to interrupt you, Loyce."

Fingers poised over the keys, jaws still rotating, Loyce looked at Lily.

"I'm here to see Woody," Lily said.

Loyce blinked. "Well, I'll tell you, Miz Trulock. We have an emergency here. You may not have heard about the murder."

Lily was stung. "I'm not deaf, dumb, and blind, Loyce."

It was a mistake. Loyce's nostrils closed a fraction. "Then you understand why Sheriff Malone can't take time out now for family matters."

Trying to sound conciliatory without feeling it, Lily said, "I wouldn't dream of coming here about family matters. I want to tell him something about the murder."

Loyce's face expressed pity for the sheriff's poor mother-in-law, reduced to pathetic attempts to be part of things by coming down and disturbing the sheriff when he was busy. Her voice was falsely sweet. "Miz Trulock, why don't you just have a seat until he's finished." She turned back to her typing.

Loyce had won. Lily turned toward the long bench that ran along the wall next to the door. For the first time, she noticed a stocky black woman sitting in the corner farthest from the door. The woman was wearing a black dress and a wide-brimmed straw hat with a black ribbon around the crown. On the bench beside her were an umbrella and a large pocketbook. She was slumped down, staring at a point on the floor in front of her feet. Lily recognized Pearl Washington, Snapper's maid.

The idea that a member of Palmetto's Negro community would, apparently voluntarily, spend time in the sheriff's office was a strange one to Lily. Surely Pearl should have been at Snapper's, where she belonged. She had even helped raise Diana. Her presence would be doubly required so she could receive, in the kitchen, condolences herself, and perhaps sympathy gifts of money slipped into the pocket of her apron. Yet there she sat, her daughter Marinda doing her job at Snapper's and being, Lily recalled, most ungracious about it.

Lily wasn't sure what to do. It would be much easier if Pearl would look her way, give some sign of recognition, but Pearl seemed unaware of her surroundings or of Lily's presence. I'll just have to go up to her, Lily thought, and she walked up to Pearl and said hello.

Pearl seemed to pull herself in. "Miz Trulock," she said heavily.

"Sad to hear about Diana."

"That poor child."

Lily saw pain in Pearl's face. "You did your best, Pearl. Everybody knows that."

"I couldn't help that child, Miz Trulock. I could talk to her sometimes, that's all. I'd rub her back and tell her a story. After a while, she'd go to sleep."

"I saw Marinda helping at Snapper's," Lily said. "I thought you'd be there."

"I would but except I had to come down here and see the sheriff." Pearl glanced at the pocketbook beside her on the bench.

"I'm waiting to see him, too. They say he's busy."

"Busy finding out who killed my gal."

Lily doubted it, but she said, "Reckon so."

Just then, Woody and Cecil burst from Woody's office, followed by a gray-haired man in dirty overalls with a goiter on his neck. At the sight of them, Pearl stood up and Lily said, "Woody—"

He ignored them both, shoving his hat on his head and saying to Loyce, "We're going after him."

"Good luck, Sheriff," Loyce shot back, and the door

banged behind Woody and Cecil before Lily could take in what had happened. The man with the goiter sketched a nod and followed them. The door closed again.

Lily looked at Pearl. "Well," she said. Pearl seemed to dissolve, as if her momentary effort had used her up.

Lily called to Loyce, "When will he be back?"

"When he's done with his business," Loyce answered, and swiveled her chair so her back was to Pearl and Lily— offended, perhaps, as much by their alliance as by the question.

Pearl sighed. "Lord, I been here two hours already."

Lily realized that Pearl would not be here at all if she didn't consider her errand extremely important. She would know that being ignored by Woody was the kindest treatment she could expect. Next would come contempt and ridicule. And, by being here instead of at Snapper's with Marinda, she was losing the wages Snapper would have paid her. Lily was curious. "Did you want to see the sheriff about Diana?"

She could see Pearl wondering whether to tell her. Having Woody walk out must have swayed the decision. "I got something seems like I need to show the sheriff," she said. "Marinda, she told me to have no more truck with it. But I think the sheriff should know." She patted her purse.

Lily nodded toward it. "It's in there?"

"Yes'm." Pearl hesitated in the face of the unasked question. "It's Miss Diana's poems."

Lily didn't know what she'd expected, but this wasn't it. "What do you mean?"

"Poems she wrote." Pearl opened her purse and withdrew a black-and-white school composition book.

The idea that Diana Landis had written poetry was so strange to Lily that she was unable to react.

"I thought the sheriff should see them, because they tell about somebody," Pearl said.

"About who?"

"I don't know who. She never told me."

"Then how do you know they tell about somebody?"

"Because I know. Because she told me about him, too."

"Him?"

"It was a man. A man she was carrying on with." Pearl tapped the book with her forefinger. "It tells about him in here, but it don't tell his name."

Lily stretched out her hand. Pearl gave her the book in an automatic movement, perhaps bred from years of handing things over when white people made gestures of wanting them.

Lily leafed through the pages. The poems were written in black ink in an unformed hand.

"Person that killed her beat her up," said Pearl. "This man, I know he nearly hit her once. She told me about it last time I saw her alive. He had a wife already. Something bad was fixing to happen. I said, 'The sheriff has got to know.' "

Something occurred to Lily. "But I thought . . ." she began, then stopped.

Pearl eyed her.

"I thought she carried on with lots of men," Lily finished, flushing.

Pearl gave a measured nod. "That was before. Before him. She used to tell me, 'Pearl, I was always looking for him, now he's found.' "

"But you don't know who he was?"

"No'm. She never said his name. She told me, 'He's got a wife. I better not say.' And she never did. My poor, dead girl." Tears oozed out of Pearl's eyes. She fumbled in her handbag and brought out a crumpled handkerchief.

Lily tried to remember if she had seen a colored person cry before. She didn't think so, except maybe on the street when the war ended. "Oh, Pearl," she said.

"She was my baby girl," said Pearl. "Mr. Snapper used to say, 'She loves you better than she loves her own granny.' "

"I'll bet she did, too," said Lily.

"She did." Pearl blew her nose. "And now I got to wait for the sheriff, or go and come back, and Mr. Snapper—"

"I'll tell you what, Pearl," said Lily.

Pearl dabbed at her eyes.

"Let me keep the book and show it to Woody. That way you don't have to take more time off. I'm his mother-in-law. He can't avoid me forever. I'll tell him just like you told me."

Pearl looked at Lily a long time, but Lily knew she would realize how sensible the suggestion was. On her own, Pearl would never have any luck with Woody, and she knew it. "All right," she said.

Lily tucked the book under her arm. "I'll tell you what he says."

Pearl picked up her umbrella from the bench. "I'll get on, then," she said.

Lily walked with her out the door and down the corridor. The few people in the halls watched curiously but without comment as they passed. They believe she's my maid, Lily thought. In trouble over a cutting or a drunk and disorderly charge. The idea was obscurely disturbing, but still it was comforting to have a pattern to fit into.

At the front door she offered Pearl a ride, and when Pearl refused she repeated, "I'll let you know about the poems."

Pearl nodded, put up her umbrella, and walked down the sidewalk, shielded from the afternoon glare. Only then did Lily remember. Pearl hadn't told Woody about the poems, but neither had Lily told him about the dark young man and the phone call. She watched Pearl's black umbrella bobbing down the street and then started toward the Nash. Sara Eubanks would be wondering what was keeping her.

Josh's Progress

All day, Josh had acted in a way that reminded him of a hog his father used to have on the farm. The hog had seemed well enough, but every now and then it would stop whatever it was doing and tremble all over—legs quivering, sides rippling, ears flapping slightly. When Josh asked why, his father chuckled and said, "Reckon he sees a ha'nt." And Josh, his belief in ghosts confirmed, watched the hog with renewed wonder. He had never understood that hog until now.

After his telephone call he had gotten back to the island early enough so Murphy's displeasure was only routine. Larry had been frying fish and hush puppies on the camp stove, the insects batting around the kerosene lanterns that hung from the branches of the trees. When he walked into camp, Josh for the first time looked down at his shirt and noticed the little smear of blood on his pocket. The trembling hadn't begun then. He unbuttoned the shirt, remarking on the heat, wadded it up, and stuffed it under his bunk in the shed. He took the obligatory swallow of moonshine, ate his fish and hush puppies with good appetite, said goodbye to Murphy when he left for his boat. And then, sitting with Amos and Larry in the yellow lantern light, Josh started to shake.

It was a slow tremor, not violent but steady. He anchored

his hands under his calves and leaned forward, trying to hold his body stable.

"You got the bellyache, boy?" said Amos. "We got to run tomorrow."

"I'm all right," said Josh. And after a while the shaking stopped.

That was the first time. Throughout the night, while he lay in his bunk in undershirt and shorts, the trembling returned at intervals. It seemed to have no relationship to what he was thinking. He didn't have to be picturing the dark-haired woman's body suspended in the murky canal, or the catfish bumping against the dead fingers. Sometimes he could think of that and be rock-steady. But then, his mind might drift to a trip he and his father and brother took to Atlanta when he was fifteen and it would start. When it did, he lay trying to turn off his mind, aware only of the rhythmic shaking that seemed to make the bunk unsteady beneath him.

Making that phone call was all he could do. And not to have a damn nickel. The woman there, talking to him, taking up time—his teeth were clenched. He relaxed his jaw, and they started to chatter. The cycle continued through the night.

The next day was worse. It was hot, the air so heavy with moisture that drawing breath was an effort. He, Amos, and Larry got the kerosene blowers going early, but it made no difference. Under the pine, the air felt a hundred degrees at least while the three of them ran the sprouted corn mash through the condenser. Josh was dizzy with the heat, the constant testing, the heavy smell. Several times, without warning, he had fits of shaking.

Toward late afternoon, Murphy arrived. His face was grave, meaty lips pursed. He inspected the day's production and nodded without enthusiasm. "We'll move it tomorrow night," was all he said. He sat on a fallen log and watched them finish. Tomorrow, they would clean the equipment and run the load of beer that was working in the barrels.

When they were done, Murphy said, "I went to the mainland today. Place is working like an anthill. Somebody got killed."

Josh was drinking a Dr. Pepper. He swallowed and asked, "Who?"

"Daughter of the congressman. Gal named Diana Landis."

"Catch who done it?" said Amos.

"Not yet. Whole damn town is in an uproar. Have to put off shipping it if things don't quieten down."

"Was she pretty?" asked Larry.

Murphy gave a rich chuckle. "I reckon she ain't too pretty *now*."

Josh swallowed the last of his drink and got up. "Maybe I'll go swimming," he said.

He got a towel from the shed and walked through the pines to the ocean, following the coastline until grass gave way to beach. There, he took off his clothes. He walked naked into the ocean, the cool water hitting him in a series of pleasant shocks, the sand soft and clean under his feet. When he was waist deep, he let his knees give way and churned himself along clumsily, like a boy raised on a farm who'd had limited contact with the water.

The salt stung his eyes. He turned onto his back, letting the swells carry him like a jellyfish. Her name was Diana. She had been killed, the spots of blood he'd found told him, aboard the *Southern Star,* the same boat he'd seen meeting Murphy's cabin cruiser yesterday morning. She was a congressman's daughter.

The current had moved him some yards down the coast. He paddled back. Diana. Had she been in the boat when he had seen it yesterday? If so, that would mean she and

Murphy were in the liquor business together, since the *Southern Star,* as Josh figured it, had delivered the payroll.

He coasted to the beach, letting the waves break over him, burying his fingers in the shifting, watery sand. A horseshoe crab, armored and ponderous, made its way along the beach. As Josh watched it, he wondered what excuse he'd give Murphy to get to the mainland this time.

At Elmore's

As the sun set, the chickens in the dirt yard of a house in the pine woods outside Palmetto gave up scratching and drifted into the chicken house to roost. A bird dog sleeping underneath the back porch worked his chin deeper into a rut in the earth and gave a slobbery sigh. The woman on the back steps shelling peas took her pan inside. In a moment, a light came on in a back window that was probably the kitchen.

Bo Calhoun watched from the scrub oak and palmetto surrounding the yard. He was sober now, surveying the homely activities with intensity, crouched in a position he had shifted only slightly in an hour.

He had awakened a while ago, drenched with sweat and his head drumming, lying across the bed fully clothed. Sue Nell had gone. He had splashed his face with water, picked through the broken glass on the living room floor, and driven out to take up his vigil.

Watching, waiting, and not moving came naturally to Bo. He had been trained to it since his earliest years. "I got four big old boys," Old Man Calhoun had always said. "I got no need to fool with anybody who ain't my kin." Stealth, a strong stomach, and a knack for glad-handing the law were requirements for the illegal whiskey trade, and as much as Old Man Calhoun could promote these characteristics in his four sons, he did so.

Deep dusk found Bo still at his post, the house still quiet. Just before dark, a car not using its headlights jounced down the dirt road and pulled up in front of the house. Bo heard the car door slam, followed by a knock and low voices. Soon, light streamed momentarily from the back door, and two men descended the steps and walked across the yard to the chicken house. They emerged carrying boxes from which came clinking sounds.

The door of the chicken house remained open. When the men disappeared around the side of the house, Bo left his hiding place, walked swiftly across the yard, and slipped inside it. A whirring restlessness among the roosting chickens was the only notice taken of him.

The car door slammed again, and the motor turned over and caught. Footsteps approached the chicken house. Bo remained motionless until a hand reached for the door. He lunged, grabbed the hand, pulled a man inside, and slammed the door amid alarmed clucks.

The man made a strangled sound as Bo's thumb pressed into his Adam's apple. Then he was necessarily silent, breathing heavily as he and Bo stared at each other.

"What say, Elmore," said Bo. He leaned close. "I want you to show me the stock you're keeping these days. If you'll do that, give me a little nod right now."

After a long moment, Elmore's head moved forward slightly, and Bo loosened his grip. "Maybe you better put some light on the subject," he said.

Elmore fumbled in his pocket, a match sparked, and a lantern hanging on a nail beside the door began to glow. In its light Elmore, a spindly, freckled, ginger-haired man in his fifties, looked greenish and drawn. His hand was shaking as he adjusted the lantern wick.

"Who was that that came by? Hosey?" asked Bo, naming the black proprietor of a juke joint in the Quarters, the Negro section of Palmetto.

Elmore cleared his throat. "Bo, what it is—"

Bo ignored him. "Let's see what you got."

Moving heavily, Elmore shifted two large sacks of chicken feed away from the wall, revealing a low door flush with the dirt floor and about a yard square. He unhooked the leather-thong latch and swung the door open. Taking the lantern from its hook, he bent to the dark cubbyhole. The lantern beam flickered off glass.

Bo took the lantern. "Bring out a sample."

Elmore crawled inside and emerged with a five-gallon glass jug filled with clear liquid. He set it on the ground near Bo's feet.

Bo squatted down, putting the lantern on the ground next to the jug. The men crouched with the jug between them, Bo rubbing his jaw and looking at the jug, Elmore looking at Bo.

The wavering light accentuated the deep hollows under Bo's eyes. The skin of his face was stretched and taut. He bent his middle finger with his thumb, released it, and gave the jug a solid thump.

The men watched bubbles rise through the liquid to rest on its top. "Nice bead," said Bo meditatively, and then, to Elmore, "Get me a jar lid."

When Elmore gave him the top of a fruit jar, Bo unscrewed the demijohn and poured some of the liquid into it. Eyes closed, he sniffed at it and sipped enough to moisten the end of his tongue. Then he set the lid on the ground and held a hand toward Elmore. Elmore dug into his pocket and gave Bo a book of matches. Bo lit one and held it to the liquid in the lid, which immediately and briefly flared into a bright flame. When it died down, Bo regarded Elmore levelly. "Over a hundred proof," he said.

Bo began to whistle between his teeth, softly and tunelessly. Elmore said, "He come by here, Bo. You'd said you'd be out of business for a while because your still blew up—"

"Whoa," said Bo. "Back up. *Who* came by?"

"Big old fellow. Not from here. He never said his name."

"And you didn't ask, either." Bo's voice was without inflection. "You didn't mind dealing with a stranger who blew up the Calhouns' still."

"He never said *he* blew up—"

"No, hell, he never said anything. Why should he? You were just as happy to deal with him no matter what he did."

"It was just that I had people to supply. Like Hosey. He was mighty put out, Bo, when I told him."

"Oh, well now," said Bo. "I'm real sorry to hear Hosey was put out. That makes the whole thing more understandable, knowing that a nigger was put out."

Bo stood up, and Elmore scrambled to his feet beside him. Bo looked at Elmore for several seconds before he spoke. "When does this big old fellow make his deliveries to you?"

"Sometimes one day, sometimes another. I can't never tell when he's—"

Bo took Elmore by the upper arms and slammed him against the wall. Elmore's head snapped back and hit with a solid thud, and he staggered to his knees. Chickens squawked, and one thrashed through the air, hit the wall, and fell motionless to the floor.

"You must want to get hurt," said Bo. "You know better than to give me that kind of trash."

"It's true," wheezed Elmore. "He don't never let me know by a day ahead."

"All right." Bo knelt beside Elmore and grasped his collar. "Next time you get the word he's coming, you let me know. If I don't hear from you, you'll hear from the Calhouns." He shook Elmore's collar gently, and Elmore's head swayed. "You hear?"

"Yes."

Bo stood and slipped out the chicken house door. Elmore didn't look up to watch him go.

Poems

Careless was the love I bore,
Careless all I'd done before.
Careless was my only song,
Careless for those I'd done wrong.
Careless until I met one
Who showed me careless days were done.
And now, 'tis true, I must confess,
That no more do I feel careless.

Lily put the composition book on the kitchen table and rubbed her eyes. The handwriting was starting to blur. Blurring, too, were the poems themselves. Diana had restricted herself to the theme of love and, however compelling it may have been for her, Lily was getting tired of it.

Lily hadn't read much poetry, but she'd read enough to know it wasn't always about love. Her own favorite poem was about a seashell. At the thought of it, she got up and went into the stuffy, little used living room where *One Hundred and One Favorite Poems* stood on the shelf next to the Bible. Back at the table, she found the place easily. "The Chambered Nautilus," by Oliver Wendell Holmes. The words slid through her head, soothing and familiar. The sea animal working its shell, its "ship of pearl," year by year in an ever-larger spiral. And at the end, the satisfying

moral: "Build thee more stately mansions, O my soul." She
read that part aloud, but not loudly enough to wake Aubrey.

Leaving Oliver Wendell Holmes, she turned back to
Diana Landis. Who could the man have been? What would
Woody make of it all, Woody who had probably never even
read "The Song of Hiawatha," much less "The Chambered
Nautilus"? She turned the page.

> *Honor thy father and mother,*
> The Bible tells us to.
> My mother is gone, my father's like stone,
> And I'd rather honor you.
>
> I didn't know it would mean choosing,
> And choosing is hard, it's true.
> But when it came to a decision,
> I knew I would have to choose you.
>
> I'd like to have honored my father
> If it hadn't been so hard to do.
> So I won't even try, just let it go by,
> And instead I'll honor you.

Sacrilege, thought Lily. It isn't funny, playing around
with the Commandments. Besides, what's all this about her
father, choosing between Snapper and this other man?
What a ridiculous whoop-te-do. Build thee more stately
mansions, O my soul.

But Diana, she reminded herself, had been young. And
Lily, she reminded herself, is not. Diana's love agonies did
bring back memories. Especially of a young man in a straw
boater who'd had amber eyes. So long ago, it was as small
and static in her mind as a panel in a love comic book. A
hint of sun behind him lit his hair when he took off his hat
. . . to greet her? To say good-bye? And that's all she could
remember. That and his name, which was David.

She closed Diana's book. She had read enough both to satisfy herself and to be fair to Pearl. Tomorrow, she would keep her promise and turn it over to Woody.

The sound of the sea was a constant faint plashing in this calm weather. She stepped onto the screened porch. The air was stirring slightly. She should be sure to listen to the weather report tomorrow. Or maybe it was her imagination.

On his cot on the porch, Aubrey stirred. The kitchen light shone dimly on his tufts of white hair, his ruddy face. He had slept out here all summer, saying that inside he couldn't get his breath and was afraid he would choke. Lily hadn't argued, hadn't known what to say. He had set up the cot, and she had put on the sheets and a light blanket, and given him his pillow from their bed. He now pulled that pillow around his ears and turned on his side. She went back into the house, where the air remained hot and unmoving, and prepared for bed. She lay a long time, watching the clouds move slowly across the moon, before she was able to sleep.

A Talk with Woody

Sara Eubanks was able to look after the store again, and Lily got an early start the next morning. In her visit with Woody, she planned as she drove toward Palmetto, she would discuss two points: the mysterious young man who made the phone call, and Diana's poems.

As she approached the courthouse, she noticed that the street was choked with cars. She didn't remember ever having difficulty finding a parking place in Palmetto before, but today she had to park down a side street two blocks away. Knots of people were standing on the courthouse lawn.

Lily, intent on her errand, wondered if there were an election rally she hadn't heard about. She soon realized, though, that her own destination was the focal point of all the attention.

The sheriff's department was jammed with people, many of them hovering around Loyce, whose jaws were grinding faster than ever. Among them Lily saw Dr. Andrews from the clinic and Brother Chillingworth. The man with the goiter who'd rushed out with Woody and Cecil yesterday was sitting on the bench eating boiled peanuts out of a damp paper bag and talking to Otis Tyree, editor of the *Palmetto Bay Observer*. In a corner stood Mrs. Chillingworth, the minister's wife, holding a large cake with coconut frosting on a cut-glass cake stand.

Lily had never cared for Mrs. Chillingworth, who in her

opinion suffered from the excessive piety that was an occupational hazard of ministers' wives. On the other hand, Mrs. Chillingworth was the only person who looked available for conversation in this unexpected crush. Lily worked her way over to where the small, rabbity-looking woman stood, and said, "What on earth is happening?"

The tip of Mrs. Chillingworth's nose reddened, and she began to cry.

"Mercy." Lily said, taking the cake stand before Mrs. Chillingworth tipped it too far and the cake slid off. "Come with me," she said, and led the weeping minister's wife out the door and down the hall to the ladies' room, where Mrs. Chillingworth sniffled and dabbed at her eyes.

Eventually, Mrs. Chillingworth got herself under control. "I am so sorry, Mrs. Trulock," she gasped. "It's just that the seminary gave that young man such a high recommendation. Even so, I know everyone will consider this a reflection on Buster."

It had never occurred to Lily to wonder if the Reverend Luke John Chillingworth had a nickname. Unable to take in "Buster," she rested the cake on the edge of the rust-stained sink.

"The bishop is sure to hear about it," said Mrs. Chillingworth. "Not that he shouldn't. Buster has nothing to condemn himself for. It's the seminary that should be worried."

"The seminary?"

"If they send murderers out as youth workers, the whole Alabama–West Florida Conference will have to change plans next summer."

The cake was listing. Lily caught it and said, "Are you talking about Wesley Stafford?"

"Of course," said Mrs. Chillingworth. She looked at the cake. "Do you think he likes coconut? I could've made chocolate. But if Wesley doesn't want it the sheriff might enjoy it. Don't you think?"

Mrs. Chillingworth peered into the mirror and patted at her hair. Lily cleared her throat. "Do you mean Wesley Stafford is supposed to have killed Diana?"

Mrs. Chillingworth glanced at Lily in surprise. "They arrested him last night. Someone saw him running away from the dock where they found her body. And I do believe I heard Buster say he'd confessed."

Numbly, Lily handed the cake back to Mrs. Chillingworth. "Confessed?"

"So Buster said." Mrs. Chillingworth smiled a wavering smile. "I'd better get back. Buster will be wondering where I am." She left, the door hissing closed behind her.

Lily remained behind, trying to take in the news. What about the dark-haired young man who hadn't had a nickel? What about Diana's poems? If Wesley had confessed, they would be meaningless. She gazed at the composition book projecting from the side pocket of her purse. She had, after all, promised Pearl.

When Lily returned, the scene in the sheriff's department was a little calmer. The Chillingworths were nowhere in sight, but the coconut cake sat on Loyce's desk. Lily had no intention of going by the rules this time. She threaded her way through the crowd and walked straight into Woody's office.

He was on the telephone, saying, "Naw, he come along just fine. Blubbered a little," when she entered. Cecil was leaning against the wall, his chair balanced on its back legs. Woody looked at her, blinked, and said into the phone, "I got to go." He hung up and turned to her. "Mother Trulock."

"Woody."

"Was there something I could quick do for you?"

Woody's face had the same look of pious inattention Lily had often seen on it in church. "There are a couple of things about the murder," she said.

Woody's eyes rolled upward slightly. "What was that?"

"Well,"—Lily pulled up a chair and sat down—"that same day, a young man came to my place all agitated. He didn't have a nickel for the phone, and—"

"You say this has something to do with the murder?"

Lily flushed. "Yes, I think so. You see, this young man—a dark young man—didn't have a nickel for the phone, and he asked me for change, and then he went and made a call and ran off. And that was about the time you got the call about the murder."

When Woody responded, his tone was exaggeratedly polite. "Mother Trulock, if you see that young man again, you tell him I want to talk to him right away, you hear?" He glanced at Cecil with the suggestion of a smile, then back at her. "Now, you said there was another thing?"

"Diana's maid gave me some poems Diana wrote. They show that Diana was carrying on with somebody. A married man."

The smile became deeper. "Do tell."

"I know she saw a lot of married men," continued Lily, her face getting hotter. "But according to the poems, this was a different type of thing."

Woody inclined his head. "I appreciate you bringing all this to my attention. Of course, now that we got Wesley Stafford apprehended, we're going to be spending most of our time looking at the evidence against him. But if we get a chance—you paying attention, Cecil?—we'll be looking into all this you've mentioned."

"You haven't even read the poems," said Lily.

"Naw ma'am, and you know what? Why don't you hang on to them for right now. Keep them real handy, in case I need them. Will you do that for me?"

Lily rose. "So nice of you to take the time." She hoped her voice conveyed adequate sarcasm.

"Glad to do it." He got up from behind his desk and ushered her toward the door.

"How did you know Wesley did it?" asked Lily.

"Gus Avery keeps the bait shack down there. He saw Wesley running away from the dock. And then Wesley confessed." From the doorway Woody indicated the man with the goiter who, alone now, was still on the bench eating peanuts.

"Did she drown?"

"Naw. Best we can figure, he tied her up and whomped her with the end of that net that had the weights in it until she died. Then he wrapped her in the net and dumped her in the drink thinking she was going to sink to the bottom. Only he didn't wait to make sure, and the net caught, and there she was."

Lily shuddered. Another thought occurred to her. She wasn't sure how to phrase it delicately. "Was she . . . had she been—you know—raped or anything?"

A flush touched the lobes of Woody's ears. "Not anything." He took her firmly by the elbow. "Thank you for coming by, Mother Trulock, and for all this good information."

Lily tried to match false heartiness with sarcasm. "And thank you, Woody, for your interest." She turned and marched out of the office.

Lily was on the courthouse lawn before she allowed her anger to surface totally. Woody thought he was so smart. She remembered how, when he was courting Wanda, he would sit outside in his car and blow the horn for her to come out. She had begged Wanda not to marry him, but Wanda couldn't see anything but to get married to the first man who came along. Wanda had probably told Woody all the bad things Lily had said about him, and he had been looking all these years for a chance to get her goat.

She'd meant to go straight back to the store. Instead, she walked across the street to Maude's Coffee Cup. She would have a glass of iced tea while she thought things over.

Josh in Palmetto

Josh didn't have to manufacture an excuse to get back to the mainland. Early in the morning, Larry discovered weevils in a five-pound bag of grits. Then a possum drowned in a barrel of mash. Josh watched Amos fish it out with a rake and fling the limp brown body into the bushes for Larry to bury since, according to him, possum was "nigger meat," not fit to be cooked for white people. After a few minutes, Josh realized that Amos was making no move to pour out the mash.

"You still going to use that?" he asked, indicating the barrel.

"Why not?"

"That possum—"

"He didn't touch hardly any of it. It's all right."

Josh gulped a mouthful of coffee, burning his lips on the tin cup.

Murphy, who had been watching, walked over to Josh. "We need some chicken wire for the top of those barrels."

"And some grits," put in Larry.

"Grits and all," said Murphy. "Might as well get it all if you're going to have to go."

Rummaging hurriedly through the supplies, Josh made a list. Murphy pulled ten dollars out of his pocket. "You can probably get it all at the store by the ferry landing, not have to go all the way into town."

Josh had no intention of going back to the store—Trulock's Grocery, was it?—where he had made the phone call. "I don't reckon they've got chicken wire, do you?"

"Maybe not. Better go to town." Murphy turned away. "Don't waste any time. We got work to do here." Josh ran for his boat.

The Palmetto municipal pier, at the edge of the city park, was a barnacle-encrusted structure that swayed over the bay on rickety pilings. In its shadow a more modern concrete dock jutted into the water, small boats moored along it at intervals. Josh tied up and started through the park toward downtown Palmetto, passing the bandstand where the candidates had sat during the fish fry. Its crepe-paper streamers stirred in the slightly moving air.

Downtown Palmetto was awakening. Shades were rolled up in the dime store's flyblown window, revealing a back-to-school display of pencils and curling notebook paper. In the drugstore, all the stools at the counter were occupied by men hunched over cups of coffee. Josh saw a sign saying *Esther's Market* and went in to buy grits.

It took longer than he expected. He had trouble finding things. The cash register at the only checkout stand stopped working, causing much speculation about what the matter was before it spontaneously repaired itself. Next door, the hardware store was possibly out of chicken wire, the clerk speculated, since Miz Johnson had replaced her whole chicken yard last week, but maybe some could be located "out back." Eventually it was. With the rolled-up wire under one arm and his bag of groceries cradled in the other, Josh emerged onto the now baking pavement.

He looked up at the courthouse clock. It was late enough. A telephone booth stood on the sidewalk in front of the courthouse. He entered it, put his purchases at his feet, and dug into his pants pocket for a nickel. This time, he had one.

When the operator came on the line, he said, "Collect to Tallahassee," and gave the number and his name. It took a few clicks before a female voice on the other end of the slightly blurry line answered, "Beverage Department," accepted the call, and said, "You all right, Josh?"

Josh allowed himself half a second to wish that he was standing in the office with her, looking out the window over the trees at the dome of the state capitol. "I need to speak to Eddie, Louise."

The phone booth was stifling. Josh mopped sweat from his forehead. A hearty voice came on the line and said, "What say, Joshua?"

"I got some problems. You know about the girl that got killed down here?"

"Congressman Landis's daughter. Yeah, it's in the papers. I heard on the radio they arrested some preacher boy."

"I didn't know that. But listen." Josh told Eddie about finding Diana Landis's body and making the call to the sheriff. "She was killed on the same boat that Murphy met that morning," he concluded. "This whole thing is connected up somehow. We got a mess on our hands."

He listened to waves of static for a while until a graver-sounding Eddie said, "Nobody knows who you are, do they, Josh? That part's all right?"

"So far so good."

"I got to check with the people upstairs. If a congressman's daughter was involved in some kind of moonshine deal and got herself killed, they may want to handle this a different way. But, for right now, your job's the same. Find out who's behind it. Is it as big an operation as we thought?"

"Big. Fancy. Kerosene blowers, so you don't see any smoke. Deep well, fancy pump. I wouldn't be surprised if they were distributing all the way to Atlanta. There's a lot of money's worth of hooch going out of there, I can tell you that."

"Plumb put the Calhouns out of business for us."

"They'll set up again. But this bunch is giving them some competition."

"Shoot. With the taxes up so nobody can afford legal liquor, every moonshiner in the country is going to be driving a Cadillac by this time next year. If we don't do something about it, that is. Eh, Josh?"

Josh rubbed his hand across his face. "That's what I'm trying to accomplish down here."

"I know. This is turning out to be a bad one. Keep after it. Call me back as soon as you can. I'll try to get to the people upstairs today."

"It isn't so easy to call. I'm stuck over on that island."

"Do the best you can, old buddy."

When Josh hung up, the inner tension that had eased while he talked with Eddie returned. His work as a revenuer had made him accustomed to being alone and, in many quarters, despised. It was his practice to go on doggedly with the job and not think about it. But seeing the dead girl yesterday had done something to him. The thought of going back to the island, of living with people he was determined ultimately to betray, made him intensely lonely. He opened the phone booth, picked up his burdens, and started slowly back toward the park, the pier, and his boat.

He was so preoccupied that he didn't glance across the street at Maude's Coffee Cup. He didn't see the woman sitting next to the window get up from a table so rapidly she upset her glass of iced tea.

Lily and Josh

By the time Lily had apologized and paid for her spilled tea, the dark young man had almost reached the corner. Moving at a half-trot, trying to look innocent—as if she'd just remembered leaving the iron on at home—she closed the distance between them.

She couldn't see his face, had seen it only in the instant he came out of the phone booth, but she was positive it was the same man who'd made the call from her store. The set of his shoulders, the curly dark hair, even the dirty khaki pants were the same.

She didn't stop to wonder what she was doing. The sight of him, after he'd been so much on her mind, made following him necessary. Woody might not care if this man had made the anonymous call about Diana's murder, but she herself, she realized now, was convinced he had. And whether or not Woody cared, she did.

The man turned toward the city park and municipal pier as Lily, now fairly close to him, followed. The narrow street was one of the oldest and least desirable residential areas in Palmetto. Many of the houses were close to tumbling down, their porch screens rusty and bowed, paint peeling from weathered boards, yards full of sandspurs and dollar weeds.

From a block away, Lily saw with consternation that Ludie Mims was sitting on her front porch. Josh was approaching her house now.

Ludie, who had passed ninety last year, spent her days in her porch swing, her feet barely touching the ground, watching with bright black eyes whoever happened along. Often, she hailed a passerby and asked for help reading a letter, claiming to have lost her spectacles. This had been going on for quite some time, and everyone in Palmetto knew the letter was a circular left in Ludie's door several years ago by the gas company. She always carried the circular in her apron pocket, and she always asked anyone who consented to read it whether it was from Charles.

Charles, Ludie's husband, had been dead for twenty years. Still, the reader, having been through the ritual before, usually thought it mannerly to say yes, it was from Charles, that Charles was doing fine and sent his love. On hearing this, Ludie would return the letter to her apron pocket, and the passerby would be free to continue.

Lily saw Ludie's head snap around when Josh walked by, and knew he was about to be caught. A rusting truck was up on blocks in the front yard next door to Ludie's. She stepped behind it. By craning her neck she could see what was happening.

"Hoo! Young man!" Ludie called.

Josh's pace slowed and he glanced Ludie's way briefly. The glance, Lily knew, was his mistake. Ludie jumped to her feet, flapped her apron at him and screeched, "Young man!"

Lily felt a flicker of approval at seeing Josh stop and realizing he was polite enough not to ignore Ludie. "Ma'am?" he said, sounding wary.

Ludie hobbled to the edge of the porch. As shrunken and stooped as she was, her voice was strong. "I need me some help."

Josh walked toward the house. "Help with what?"

"This here letter." Ludie removed it from her pocket and waved it at him. "I need to read it, and I can't find my spectacles."

Lily saw Josh hesitate, then lift his shoulders in evident resignation, set his groceries and chicken wire on the front walk, and take the letter. He unfolded it and stood reading while Ludie watched. "Is it from Charles?" she asked.

He glanced at Ludie, then back at the letter. "Well, no'm," he said finally. "It's from the West Florida Gas Company, wanting to know if you could use—"

"But is it from *Charles*?" persisted Ludie.

"—a new dryer. A gas dryer."

Josh and Ludie regarded one another.

Lily saw Ludie straighten as much as she could with her back the way it was. "What does Charles say?" she asked.

Josh glanced back at the paper, then at Ludie again. He refolded the paper and handed it to her. "He says he's just fine. Sends his regards."

Ludie returned the paper to her pocket. Before Josh could turn away she said, "What's your name, young man?"

"Josh."

"Where do you stay at?"

Lily moved closer as Josh said, "Just visiting."

"But where do you stay at?" Ludie's voice got louder as Josh backed away.

"Not around here."

"The island?"

"Well—"

"You got to watch out on that island." Ludie started down her front steps. "There's chiggers as big as horseflies. Charles went over there hunting once, they like to eat him up. Had to bathe him and the dog in turpentine when they got home."

"Yes'm." Josh scooped up his bundles.

"You got your boat down to the pier, I reckon. Won't take more than half an hour to get over there. That about right?"

"I never said—"

"Where you staying at over there? The Elmo House? Best creamed corn I ever did eat, when Charles and I went over there on a Sunday. The lady that runs it, Miss Rose, she still there?"

"I don't—"

Lily thought of the Elmo House as it was now, boarded up for years, sand sifting through cracks in the windows and crabs scuttling across the front porch.

Josh was backing down the street nodding good-bye to Ludie.

Ludie's right, thought Lily. He's staying on the island.

She waited until Josh turned around and Ludie was struggling back up her steps, then slipped by Ludie's house. Josh was deep among the pines and azaleas of the overgrown park, but Lily no longer cared about catching up with him.

A motor sputtered and came to life. By the time she reached the pier he was a blot on the green water. A blot moving, she noted as she stood shading her eyes, directly toward the southern end of St. Elmo.

Lily Visits Wanda

Lily leaned against the railing of the pier. The young man—Josh, he had told Ludie his name was—had made the anonymous call and told Woody where to find Diana's body. She was sure of it. But how would he have known? He had been up to something. Maybe he killed Diana himself. Maybe he was a man she ran into somewhere and treated mean. He might've been the one who wouldn't stand for it.

But Woody had said Wesley confessed to killing her. Lily thought of Wesley in his choir robe, his hair bristling, his Adam's apple bobbing as the choir struggled through "His Eye Is on the Sparrow." Wesley and his tract about lust. Wesley admiring the *Island Queen*. Her eyes burned from the dazzle of the water, and she turned away. Religious fanatics had caused a lot of trouble in the world before now, she knew. But Wesley had always seemed more pitiful than dangerous.

She wandered back toward her car. Now that she was in town, she supposed she ought to visit Wanda. She contemplated her daughter without enthusiasm. Something had gone wrong between her and Wanda. Perhaps it was Wanda's insistence on marrying Woody. That had been ten years ago, and since then they had fallen into a routine that could barely pass for intimacy. And now with Aubrey the way he was, who did she have left? Lily blinked the thought away as she slid into the baking-hot Nash. Wanda would know the sheriff's department gossip about the murder, and that was good enough reason to visit.

Wanda and Woody lived in a raw-looking house in what once had been planned as a subdivision. The developers had found, however, that few Palmetto citizens were interested in moving from town to the sandy, blistered, shadeless lots of Palmetto Heights. Only a handful of flat-roofed, pastel-painted stucco houses had been built before the project was abandoned. Woody had bought one, so Wanda lived surrounded by an acre of sandspurs with no water, not even a stream, in sight. Lily wondered how she could stand it.

As she turned into the driveway, she realized it was getting toward noon, and hoped Woody would be too busy to come home and eat dinner. She had seen enough of him for one day.

Wanda was wearing shorts and a sleeveless blouse, her legs and arms looking white and thin. Her brown hair was in pincurls with a bandanna tied around it. She invited Lily into the shadowy living room, the venetian blinds angled against the sun. An ironing board was set up on the back breezeway, and on a table next to it the radio was murmuring.

"I was just about to have some Jell-O. Would you like some?" Wanda's offer was listless.

The Jell-O was lime, with fruit cocktail suspended in it, and it started to form a green puddle as soon as it was put on the saucer. Wanda served it with saltines and a dot of mayonnaise on top. Over that and iced tea, Lily learned that her grandson was enjoying second grade. When the subject was exhausted, Lily said, "Guess Woody's been busy, with Diana Landis getting murdered."

"Palmetto will be a better place with her gone."

Wanda seemed to expect life to be as spotless as the rooms pictured in fancy magazines. "Diana had troubles, just like the rest of us," Lily said, distressed by the admonitory tone in her own voice.

"She certainly has caused Woody enough trouble."

"How? He's arrested Wesley, hasn't he?"

Wanda's mouth was tight. "Yes he has, and thank goodness. Now maybe things can settle down."

"Has Snapper been rough on Woody?"

"Not really. He even refused absolutely to use his pull in Tallahassee to get any help with the investigation. Woody was gratified. But Woody was walking on eggs the whole time. All he had to do was rub Snapper the wrong way. . . ." Wanda's voice trailed off at the image of Woody's wrecked career.

Lily remembered Snapper's expressed faith in Woody's ability as a lawman. But Woody had never investigated a murder before. "Is Snapper satisfied it was Wesley?"

"Seems to be. What Snapper's really thinking about, Woody says, is the election, because now he's sure to win."

"How's that?"

"Diana was costing him votes, and now she's gone. It gets his name all over the papers, too. There was a reporter from Tallahassee here, and somebody may even come up from Jacksonville. Snapper can run for senator next time, Woody says."

Lily crumbled a saltine. "How did Woody know that Wesley did it?"

"That little fellow that sells bait? Gus Avery? The one with the thing on his neck? He'd been off fishing and come back, and he saw Wesley high-tailing it away from the *Southern Star* and into the woods. He didn't think much about it then, because Diana usually had men around, so he went on home. When he heard she'd been killed, he told Woody."

"Woody tracked Wesley down?"

"Didn't have to. Went to his rooming house and there he was, with his Bible on his knees, reading about the whore of Babylon. He practically fell all over Woody to tell him he killed her."

"Did he say why?"

Wanda's cheeks colored. "No. But you can just about bet she tried to get him to do something—you know."

Lily knew, and in fact it sounded plausible. Why, then, did the young man named Josh still seem so important? "Did Woody find out who made that call? The anonymous one?"

"Woody figures it was just somebody passing who didn't want to get slowed down. Would you like a piece of pound cake?"

Lily left Wanda ironing Woody's uniforms and listening to "The Romance of Helen Trent." The store, dusty and quiet as it was, looked like a haven. She paid Sara Eubanks and sat on a stool behind the counter, glad for a glimpse of the bay through the screen door.

She wondered if anyone on the island knew the man named Josh. She needed some more nets from Sam Perry. It wouldn't hurt to go over there one day soon, and—

The screen door flew open, and a group of children banged in, shouting about candy.

Wesley Incarcerated

Whatever Lily was going to do about Josh, it would have to wait for another day. In the meantime, her thoughts turned to Wesley again and again during the long, sleepy afternoon. He might have killed Diana, but he had also stood beside Lily and admired the *Island Queen,* and she had felt in that moment that he wasn't a complete fool. He would need more than Mrs. Chillingworth's cake to let him know somebody was thinking about him.

She told Aubrey at supper. When she explained about Wesley's being in jail and ended, casually, "So I thought I'd drive in to see him this evening," Aubrey's reaction surprised her.

"What for?" he said, marking the first time in months he had asked her a question.

She was almost too astonished to reply. "Just to . . . you know, see how he is, maybe take him something," she fumbled.

"Boy killed somebody. Better stay away," Aubrey said, and reached for another corn muffin.

Lily was in a dilemma. Aubrey had shown a slight concern for her welfare. To encourage him, surely she should give in and do as he advised. What difference did it make if she went to see Wesley or not? Yet she knew, as sure as she was sitting there, that she meant to go ahead with her plan.

"I won't stay but a minute," she said, and Aubrey finished eating in silence.

The courthouse was locked, and the entrance to the jail around back was dark and forbidding. Clutching a few back issues of the *Saturday Evening Post* and a bar of lavender soap for Wesley, Lily approached the dimly lit concrete stoop. Through the screen door she could see a desk and, seated at it, Deputy Cecil Barnes. Wesley was too important, she judged, to be guarded by the regulars, most of whom would, so Lily had heard, turn their backs on anything if you gave them a pack of chewing gum.

Cecil was cleaning his fingernails with an attachment on his pocket knife. He looked up when Lily entered, and his voice registered surprise when he said, "Good evening, ma'am."

"Evening," said Lily. "I've come to visit Wesley Stafford."

"Well now, ma'am. . . ."

Lily had anticipated that whoever was watching Wesley wouldn't want to let her see him. She was prepared for stronger opposition than Cecil Barnes could offer. She had the advantage with Cecil because one Christmas years ago she had caught him stealing a peppermint candy cane and promised not to tell his daddy if he wouldn't do it again.

"I have some things I want to give him," she said, displaying the soap and magazines, "and I thought," she added in sudden inspiration, "he might want to join me in a word of prayer."

Having conferred on herself semiofficial status from the Lord, Lily had no doubt that Cecil's next move would be to get out the keys. In fact, he did. "Come on in here, ma'am," he said, unlocking the door to the cells.

The Palmetto jail had two cells at the end of a short corridor. In one, the bunk was occupied by a profoundly motionless figure. In the other, crouched on the floor near the bars, where the corridor light could reach the leaves of his open Bible, was Wesley. His lips were moving. He didn't look up when Cecil said, "Miz Trulock's here to visit."

"Hello, Wesley," Lily said.

In the subdued light, Wesley's face looked knobby. A smudge darkened his cheek, and one lens of his glasses, Lily saw, was cracked.

"What happened to him?" she asked Cecil.

"Resisted arrest a little."

"I thought he confessed."

"He did, pretty much." Cecil stood watching Wesley.

"I'm not here to help him escape," said Lily. "You can leave us alone for a word of prayer."

Cecil bobbed his head and returned down the corridor. Lily knelt outside the bars and said, "Wesley." She shoved the *Saturday Evening Post*s toward him. "I brought you some magazines." He didn't respond, and after a moment she held out the bar of soap. "And some soap."

Wesley swayed forward. *"Save me, O God,"* he said, *"for the waters are come in unto my soul."*

Wesley's voice had always been rich and full, his best feature. Now harsh with anguish, it had an eerie power. If he could only preach now, Lily thought, he'd convert all of Palmetto.

"I'm sorry," she began, but he wasn't listening.

"I sink in deep mire, where there is no standing: I am come into deep waters, where the floods overflow me."

As always when she heard the psalm, Lily thought King David must have known a place much like Palmetto. She, too, had seen deep mire, deep waters, floods. She understood what it meant for the waters to enter your soul, or thought she did. She reached through the bars and touched Wesley's shoulder.

He looked at her. "It's me, Lily Trulock," she said. "I brought you something."

She could see no recognition in his eyes. He drew a breath and said, *"I am weary of my crying: my throat is dried: mine eyes fail while I wait for my God."*

He was crazy. Lily felt cold, confronted with it. Wesley's face, however, seemed to burn. He clutched at her sleeve, pulling her close enough to feel his breath as he continued the psalm, dropping his voice to a fervent half-whisper. *"They that hate me without a cause are more than the hairs of mine head: they that would destroy me, being mine enemies wrongfully, are mighty: then I restored that which I took not away."* She felt his hand shaking. "That which I took not away, Miss Lily."

One of his eyes seemed weirdly divided by the broken lens of his glasses. "You know me, then," she said.

He turned back to the Bible and read, *"Deliver me out of the mire, and let me not sink: let me be delivered from them that hate me, and out of the deep waters."*

Kneeling there with the smell of lavender faint in her nostrils from the soap she still held, Lily felt dizzy. What was Wesley telling her? *I restored that which I took not away.* Could that mean confessing to something you hadn't done? "Did you kill Diana?" she whispered.

He closed his eyes and once again his lips moved soundlessly. Although she remained minutes longer, he didn't look up or speak again. She got to her feet and left him.

Cecil was cleaning a rifle, the parts spread on a white dish towel on the desk. "See all you wanted?" he asked with the suggestion of a smirk.

"How did Woody get the idea he killed Diana?"

Cecil ticked off on his fingers. "Feller seen him running from the boat. We went to his rooming house. He's there reading his Bible and crying. He tells us he done it."

"How'd his glasses get broken?"

Cecil was shamefaced. "He run off. I had to stop him. But when the sheriff asked him if he'd killed her, Miss Lily, he says, 'Yes, God forgive me,' and cries harder." Cecil's face had a mulish look, and Lily didn't argue.

Aubrey was asleep on his porch cot when she got home. She took the Bible from its shelf and turned to the sixty-ninth psalm, in which King David complains of his afflictions and prays for deliverance. She read it through. Wesley was asking me to help him, she thought. *Deliver me out of the mire,* he had said, *and let me not sink.* But what could she do? The dark face of the man named Josh came into her mind. He knew something about the murder. She had already planned to see what she might find out about him. Would that help deliver Wesley out of the mire? Was it, in any case, her business to deliver him?

Maybe it wasn't. But Woody, she knew, would never admit that Wesley might not be the murderer. Snapper was satisfied. She was the only one who cared.

Poor Wesley, she thought, with his Bible and his broken glasses. He was in the psalm, too. She ran her finger down until she found the verse, which was addressed to the Lord: *For the zeal of thine house hath eaten me up.*

Preparations

Bo Calhoun was making preparations. He ignored Sue Nell, who had returned from the fish camp early that morning saying she had some things to pick up. She watched him oil his shotgun and then oil it again a few hours later. He had talked on the telephone with each of his brothers and now, in the late afternoon, the four of them were gathered on the front porch drinking beer. Their conversation drifted through the open window into the living room, where Sue Nell sat on the floor, sorting through a tackle box.

The children were still at Sonny's. Sonny's wife, Missy, with every appearance of disapproval, had offered to keep them for a few days. "Until your nerves are better," she said to Sue Nell.

"I don't reckon I'll ever have as much nerve as you do," Sue Nell shot back, and Missy retaliated by offering to have the doctor look at the rash on Little Bo's legs, which really shouldn't have been let go so long.

"You left. Why the hell didn't you stay gone," was all Bo had said when Sue Nell walked in.

"I'll be gone soon enough," she said.

That had been right before the call came from Elmore. After the call, Bo didn't speak to Sue Nell at all, but went ahead with his planning as if she weren't there. She, for her part, packed a cardboard box with an assortment of supplies: clothes, canned goods, and a lump of lead for making weights for a net and the mold to make them with, corks and fishing line, a ten-pound sack of corn meal, a nickel-plated pistol with a bone handle. Arrayed on the floor in front of her was a tangle of fish hooks. She sorted them by size with her forefinger. Her red hair clung damply to her neck.

Bo's voice surged with energy. "He comes up the canal in a cabin cruiser. Elmore will be at the entrance to the slough at eight o'clock to meet him. You all be there at seven. Park on the fire road and come up over the ridge."

There were murmurs of agreement and a shuffling as the men got to their feet. Then Lester's voice, thin with excitement or fear: "What about Daddy?"

"We'll tell him afterward."

The voices faded as they walked down the steps, Bo accompanying them to their cars.

The hooks were sorted, largest to smallest, in a neat line. Sue Nell scooped them up, undoing all her work, and dropped them into an empty metal Band-Aid can. She stood up and put the can in her cardboard box briskly, with the air of someone who has made a decision.

Ambush

Josh felt uneasy, watching the mainland come closer. Venturing into unfamiliar territory without knowing what to expect wasn't his style, and Murphy's order that he help make the delivery tonight had been unexpected. His task, Murphy had said, would be to transfer cartons of liquor from the boat to a truck. That was all. As long as he didn't break anything, it sounded simple. He glanced sidelong at Murphy, who was driving the boat. Murphy's blubbery profile looked grim in the fading light.

They passed the ferry landing, the pilings stark in the twilight. A few more miles down the coast, the cruiser made a right-hand arc into the mouth of the canal.

Here it was darker, the tall cypresses cutting off much of the last light. There was a brackish smell of mud and rotting leaves, and overhead a flock of birds wheeled through their last arc of the evening. Josh, straining his eyes ahead, was the first to see the shadowy outline of a bateau in the middle of the canal. He sat forward. There was a figure standing up in the boat waving a flashlight.

"Watch it," he said. To go around either end of the boat would be to risk knocking a hole in the cruiser's bottom on cypress knees. Murphy cursed and cut the motor while Josh scrambled out on deck.

"Hey," he called. "Did your motor conk out?"

The flashlight went off, but the figure didn't answer at first. As the cruiser drifted closer a female voice said, "I've got something to tell you-all."

They were close enough now to converse normally. "Something to tell who?" Josh's mouth filled with saliva, and he wished suddenly and violently for his shotgun.

"You're going to meet Elmore, aren't you?" said the voice.

"Just a minute." Josh returned to the cabin and said to Murphy, "It's some lady, says she has something to tell us if we're heading to meet Elmore."

Murphy grunted, picked up his shotgun from the rack, and went on deck. Josh trailed behind. "What was it you wanted to say?" Murphy asked.

"Don't go there," said the woman. "Somebody's there waiting for you."

Murphy rubbed his belly for a moment, then said, "Ma'am, head over to the bank and tie up. I'd like to talk to you."

There was the gargle of a small motor being cranked—not more than five horsepower, Josh guessed—and the bateau slid toward the bank. As Murphy started the cruiser and followed, Josh saw the figure tie up to some bushes, then come to the back end of her boat and wait for the cruiser to drift alongside. When it did, she grabbed the ladder and climbed up, disregarding the hand Josh offered to help her on deck.

From what he could see in the dusk, she was skinny and wore pedal pushers, a sleeveless blouse, and sandals. Her long hair, frizzing in the evening humidity, was pulled to the nape of her neck. "You were about to get your ass shot off, boy," she said.

Josh was unsure how to respond. "Come on in here," he said, indicating the cabin.

She followed him, and Murphy greeted them with a nod, then said to Josh, "I'm heading up that creek a little ways. Get out there and drop the anchor."

When the boat was anchored in a winding slough the three met in the cabin. Murphy stood in the doorway with the shotgun cradled in his arm. Josh lit a lantern, and in its light he could see that the woman's hair was dark red. She had a strong chin, which was thrust forward, and she stood with her legs apart, looking from one to the other of them.

"Now, what are you talking about?" said Murphy.

"My husband and his brothers are waiting for you. They plan to hurt you bad."

The answer was so prompt and sharp that Josh thought Murphy seemed taken aback. "What for?"

"He figures you blew up his still and stole his business."

Murphy sat on the edge of the bunk and pinched the bridge of his nose between finger and thumb. "Who the hell are you?"

"Sue Nell Calhoun."

The Calhouns, Josh thought. I was afraid of this. Sue Nell, he noticed, looked highly stimulated. She moved jerkily around the cabin, the corners of her mouth curving upward. Although he knew he should let Murphy do the talking, a question escaped him: "Why are you telling us?"

She glanced at him. "Reasons."

"I tell you what, little lady," said Murphy, getting up. "I think I better have a look at what's going on up there. And while I do, I think you better stay here with my boy Josh." He rubbed the back of his neck meditatively, then turned back to Sue Nell. "I'm going to take your boat back to the landing." He said to Josh, "I got a truck parked there."

Sue Nell nodded. "If you go up the fire road you'll see some Oldsmobiles. That's them. But you better not get too close, or you'll be sorry."

Murphy motioned for Josh to join him on deck. Outside,

he said, "If she's telling the truth, I got to let somebody know. She don't go anywhere until I get back."

"All right," said Josh. Murphy took up the anchor, and Josh drove the cruiser back to the canal and Sue Nell's bateau. He heard a thump as Murphy landed in it. As he swung the large boat back toward the creek, he saw Murphy's dark form heading the bateau toward the mouth of the canal. He anchored in the creek again and returned to the cabin.

Sue Nell had kicked off her sandals and was looking in Murphy's ice chest. "Thought maybe there'd be a beer," she said.

Josh shook his head.

"There must be moonshine, then," she said. "That's why you're in this mess, isn't it?"

"We got some liquor on board. You saying you want some?"

"Don't go to any trouble."

Without responding to the sarcasm, Josh went to the stack of cartons against the wall and removed a demijohn. He found two glasses in the cupboard, poured each half full, and gave one to her. They drank in silence, Josh listening to the water slapping the sides of the boat and listening, too, for any unusual noises. The whole thing might be a trick. A plot to hijack the boat and the whiskey.

He looked at Sue Nell. She was sitting on the bunk, feet tucked under her. She wasn't pretty at all. Scrawny, with a yellowish pale face, freckles, and eyes like swamp water. Frizzy red hair coming loose. Just the type to be lying, and now Murphy had left him here alone. He climbed up to the steering cabin, took his shotgun from the rack, and returned, feeling better.

Sue Nell watched him over the rim of her glass. "You going to shoot me?"

Josh didn't reply. He propped the gun next to him. Most of his drink was gone. He'd better take it slow.

She held out her glass for a refill. "My husband makes better whiskey than that."

Pride of workmanship overrode Josh's caution. "If your husband makes such good whiskey, why are you here? Why aren't you helping him shoot us to pieces?"

"I didn't come here because he makes bad liquor."

"Why, then?"

"He does other bad things." She swallowed deeply from the glass he handed her, and Josh thought he saw her eyelids droop.

"He'll be mad, if he finds out what you did."

"Oh hell. Let him be mad. I don't even live with him anymore."

"Why not?"

"None of your business?"

"Where do you live?"

"None of your business."

Josh sipped his drink. He had no head for moonshine. He didn't like Sue Nell Calhoun. It was likely to be a long time before Murphy got back. Josh would've given a lot to know who he was going to see, and he might've been able to find out if it wasn't for being stuck with Sue Nell. A wave of anger filled him with his next swallow. "You're something," he said. "I'm glad you're not married to me."

She looked him over swiftly and said, "So am I."

Sue Nell hummed a few bars of "The Tennessee Waltz," got to her knees, and looked out the window. "Wonder where your big old ugly friend is."

"Don't you worry about it."

"Keeps you hopping, does he, calls you 'my boy Josh,' tells you what to do?"

Josh said nothing. "I'm thirsty," she said, holding out her glass.

Josh refilled it and his own. She looked at him speculatively. "Where you from?"

"Near Columbus."

"Georgia boy. That explains a lot."

"Like what?"

"About your personality and all. Bet you grew up on a farm."

"What if I did?"

Sue Nell snickered. "I could tell, that's all."

Strands of her hair were escaping from the rubber band. I would like to take and snatch that red hair out, Josh thought. I would like to give this lady a clip up beside the head, just enough to shut up that smart mouth. He said, "I guess Georgia people aren't nearly as nice as Palmetto people. We don't even hardly ever beat up girls and kill them."

Sue Nell sat very still. "That's what you folks do, isn't it," he went on recklessly. "Murder your own congressman's daughter? Nice people."

"Maybe you ought not to mouth off so much about something you don't know about." Her voice was harsh.

The blood rushed to Josh's face. "And how do you know what I know about and what I don't? Maybe I know more about it than you think."

They glared at each other. At that moment, it struck Josh forcibly that with her face flushed, making her eyes look gold, Sue Nell didn't look so bad. Her mouth, which he hadn't noticed before, struck him as being particularly soft and pink.

As he watched, her lips began to quiver. It seemed an effort for her to form the words, "What do you mean?"

"Nothing. Never mind," said Josh. "Did you know the girl or something?"

Her expression didn't change, but he saw that she was shaking. The liquid left in her glass sloshed, and it took both her hands to steady it.

He picked up his drink and went to sit beside her on the bunk.

"I'm sorry," said Josh. "Was she a friend of yours?"

Her lips twisted. "No friend of mine. My husband's lover."

"Oh Lord."

Without thinking, he put his arms around her. She pulled back at first, but then he saw her eyes change. She leaned forward and rested her head against his shoulder.

Josh stroked her hair. The palms of his hands felt warm. "It's bad. Real bad," he said, not sure what he was referring to. She didn't answer. "You saved us," he said.

She sat up and looked at him solemnly. Josh saw drops of perspiration clinging to the fine hairs above her upper lip. She swayed a little, her eyes dilated. "I saved you. Don't forget that," she said.

Josh ran a finger over the knob of her ankle. "I been on that island, nobody to talk to," he said. "We live in a shed, nothing but a shed. There's bugs." He closed his eyes, trying to remember what he had meant to say. "Nothing but a shed," he said. The words filled him with such sadness that his eyes prickled.

He felt her palm cradle his cheek. "At least you're free," she said.

He turned to her. "I'm not," he said. "There's Murphy first, and then there's—" Her mouth was close to his, so close he couldn't read her eyes. When he kissed her, she tasted faintly of salt. He felt a rush of yearning so strong that before it engulfed him a small, separate part of his mind was dismayed. Minutes later, when he ran his hand over her small breasts, he said, "Oh God." Sue Nell said nothing.

Josh had been with an assortment of women, but Sue Nell displayed an abandon that was outside his experience. It made him feel craving mixed with fear, as if he might be swallowed up and lost.

When it was over, he said, "I have to see you. Where do you live?"

Sue Nell shook her head.

"I mean it," said Josh. "Even if you don't tell me, I'll find you."

"Why?"

Josh wasn't sure himself. "I need to see you."

Her eyes narrowed. "There's a fish camp on Tupelo Branch. That's where I'm staying. I'm telling you because I don't want you asking about me, not because I want you coming around."

Josh took her by the shoulders and kissed her hard. Now he knew he would see her again.

Murphy's Visit

Pearl Washington regarded Murphy across the kitchen table. On the table was a silver tray laden with china cups and saucers, silver spoons and linen napkins. "It's a prayer meeting," she said. "They're praying for Miss Diana."

Murphy drummed his fingers on the tabletop. "When will they be through praying?"

"I don't know."

Murphy got up and walked around the room. He peered out the window. Pearl sliced thin slices of banana nut bread and arranged them on a plate.

"Is that coffee I smell?" asked Murphy.

Pearl raised her eyebrows and pointedly ignored the china cups. She took a crockery mug from a cabinet, filled it with coffee from the twenty-cup coffee maker on the counter, and handed it to Murphy.

He drank it leaning against the counter. When he was finished, he said, "God dog it, I've got to talk to him."

"You can't walk in in the middle of a prayer. The preacher's there. Everybody."

Murphy looked at her shrewdly. "*I* can't walk in there. What about you? You got to take that truck"—he indicated the tray—"in there sometime."

"Not till Mr. Snapper tells me."

"To hell with that. Go get him."

Pearl folded her arms and stood still.

Murphy crossed the room and gripped her arm. "You get your butt in there and tell him Murphy's here. If you don't, I'm going to hurt you."

Pearl's eyes flickered. She picked up the tray and pushed through the swinging door that separated the kitchen from the dining room. In a few minutes she returned empty-handed. "He's coming," she said.

Snapper pushed into the room on a waft of hair oil. He was wearing a dark suit and a stiffly starched white shirt. His normally full, ruddy face hung in pale folds. "What the hell is going on?" he said.

"The Calhouns know," said Murphy. "They was waiting for us on the canal. Only reason we didn't run into them was Bo Calhoun's wife stopped us."

Snapper sat down at the table. "Give me a cigarette," he said to Pearl.

When he'd lit a Lucky from the pack Pearl gave him out of the kitchen drawer, he said, "Goddamn it, I've got a room full of folks out there reading the Bible." He looked at Murphy. "If anybody finds out about this, there goes the election."

"Nobody knows I'm here," Murphy said.

"Damn the Calhouns."

"Blowing up their still made them mad. I told you they wouldn't quit."

"Well, hell, I knew they wouldn't quit. But we needed a head start, a little slack." Snapper broke off and rubbed his hands over his slicked-back hair. "How the hell did they find out?"

Murphy helped himself to another cup of coffee. "My guess is they got to Elmore. He hasn't got any sand in his craw. We shouldn't have tried to take over the Calhouns' people."

"But Elmore doesn't know where the still is. He doesn't know about me."

"Naw."

Snapper said, "This operation has cost me more grief and more money than anything I ever got into. Money for supplies. Setup expenses. Salaries. And no sooner do we get the damn thing working good than this happens."

Murphy rubbed his belly and looked vacantly out the window.

"Listen to me," said Snapper. "I got a daughter lying in the funeral home graveyard dead. I got an election where some pious son of a bitch is making me hop. I got a prayer meeting in my front room. And now I got this mess."

He ground out his cigarette and stood up. "You get this shored up," he told Murphy. "If you don't, I'm not the only one who's in trouble. You shore it up, and then you let me know. And don't come waltzing in here any time you feel like. Give me a little warning next time."

Murphy nodded. He left by the back door.

When he was gone, Snapper turned to Pearl. "I got to get back for the benediction. Give me five minutes, and then come pour the coffee."

Aftermath

The moon shone on the canal, casting a track on the murky water, but under the moss-hung trees the bank was dark. There was no sound aside from the shuffle of small animals or the calling of owls.

Bo Calhoun stirred on the rotten log where he had been sitting, shotgun across his knees, for the better part of three hours. Beside him sat Elmore. An hour before, Elmore had slumped forward and put his head in his hands, and he hadn't moved since. Bo took a breath, whistled through his teeth, and called, "Come on out, boys."

Three shadowy figures emerged from the trees. Bo joined them, Elmore trailing behind. Sonny and Purvis lit cigarettes, the matches brief points of flame in the dark.

Sonny expelled smoke and massaged the back of his neck. "Nothing but a water haul. Useless trip." he said.

"Damn right." Bo's voice was neutral. He turned to Elmore. "You got anything to say?"

Elmore swallowed. "I don't know. I done just like you said. It was all set."

"They always showed up before?"

"Yeah, sure, but I don't know what happened this time." Elmore twisted his knobby hands together. "I didn't warn them, Bo."

Bo leaned his shotgun against a tree and turned back to Elmore. "Somebody told them. Nobody knew about it except my brothers and you. Are you telling me I can't trust my own brothers?"

"I didn't warn them, Bo."

When the openhanded blow landed on the side of Elmore's head, the sound was loud enough to rouse a faint echo from across the canal. Elmore staggered, his head bent. The moonlight caught moisture dripping from his nose. Bo jerked Elmore's head upright. "Somebody had to tell," he said. "Otherwise, how'd they know not to come?"

Elmore tried to shake his head, and Bo hit him again. "Answer me."

"I swear to God . . . I never told—I don't know his name—he has a cabin cruiser . . . big old boy. . . ." Elmore's words were lost in a wheeze.

Bo picked up his shotgun and placed the muzzle under Elmore's chin. Elmore gagged. "You're going to find out for me where I can get that fellow," Bo said. "Do you understand?" He prodded with the shotgun.

"I'll find out," Elmore gasped.

"If you don't, I'll know you messed me up tonight."

"I didn't. I swear."

Bo lowered the gun. "Get on," he said, and Elmore, shoulders sagging, walked off through the trees. The brothers stood until they heard a motor come to life and then fade as Elmore drove his truck away.

"You shouldn't have let him go," said Purvis. "He told them about tonight. He probably knows where to find them right now."

"No he doesn't. Not if they've got any sense," said Bo. "Let him think it over. He can't get away from us. And he knows I'm itching to destroy his skinny ass."

The Calhouns trudged heavily through the swamp to the fire road, a narrow track along which their cars were parked. After bidding his brothers good night, Bo drove toward the beach. He turned into the parking lot of Sal's Roadhouse.

Conversation with Elmore

Josh sat in Murphy's pickup, gazing out the window at the moonlit pines. Beside him, Murphy slouched lower in his seat. "Sons of bitches waited a long time," Murphy said.

Josh grunted. Sue Nell had said she was staying at a fish camp on Tupelo Branch. He could find Tupelo Branch on the nautical chart once they were back on the boat. His need to know where she was made his forehead feel tight. Once he found Tupelo Branch he could find her, if he had to visit every shack.

He and Sue Nell had been dressed and sipping another drink by the time Murphy returned. Murphy glanced at the glasses and said, "Got into the stock, I see."

"Being sociable," said Josh.

"Miz Calhoun is welcome to a drink. She done us a big favor. They was waiting down there, just like she said." He turned to Sue Nell. "We got some more business to do. Maybe you better get on now."

Sue Nell got up without hesitation and without a glance at Josh. He followed her on deck and helped her into her bateau. He whispered fiercely, "I got to see you." She didn't reply.

Tupelo Branch. He would find it on the chart. He would get Murphy to let him away from the still somehow, and he would go there.

"Here he comes," said Murphy. "Get out."

Josh slid rapidly out of his side of the truck, leaving the door open. Murphy did the same. Josh stumbled on the hard, rutted clay of the road as the two of them ran, heads down, from their hiding place toward the dark house. A truck pulled up in front of the house and its motor cut off as Josh reached the edge of the yard. Murphy passed him, and Josh could hear the large man's labored breathing. He hadn't realized Murphy could move so fast.

The door on the driver's side of the truck started to open. Murphy wrenched it wide. "Get him," he said to Josh.

Josh reached in and pulled Elmore from behind the wheel. Elmore didn't resist, but went limp in Josh's grasp and fell to his knees in the dirt. Kneeling beside him, Josh saw blood smeared on his upper lip. "I couldn't help it," Elmore gasped. "They was going to kill me."

Murphy jerked him to his feet. "I ought to kill you myself."

"No!" said Elmore. "Help me."

"Help you," said Murphy. "I was helping you plenty. You got a hell of a lot bigger cut from us than the Calhouns ever gave you. And you pay me back by selling me out."

"Bo knew. You promised he wouldn't know."

Murphy looked at Josh. "Let's go. We got to find a distributor with some guts."

Elmore plucked at Murphy's shirt. "Bo's going to kill me. You got to help me. Don't let him kill me."

"What do I care if he kills you? You're nothing but scum to me. But I'll tell you this—" Murphy took Elmore's upper arms and pulled him forward. "If you ever say anything more about this operation to anybody, you won't have to be scared of Bo Calhoun anymore. You'll be too busy being scared of me."

He loosened his grip, and Elmore sagged backward. "You mean I ain't going to distribute for you no more?" His voice was thin.

"I don't deal with lying, two-timing scum."

"But I want. . . ." Elmore's voice trailed off as Murphy motioned with his head to Josh and turned away.

They were silent on the drive back to the mouth of the canal. Murphy spoke only to say, "No point in running again till I get this straight."

"Yeah," said Josh. His heart lurched. If the still wasn't running, he could find Tupelo Branch.

He was in the cabin of the boat, reaching for the nautical chart, when he thought he saw something moving under the trees. He squinted. Murphy started the motor. Josh picked up a flashlight and unrolled the chart. With any luck at all, he could find it before Murphy got curious enough to ask him what he was doing.

Lily Goes to the Island

A green wake spread out behind the Trulocks' boat as Lily turned it toward St. Elmo. The little swells washed against the pilings of the ferry landing where Aubrey stood. Lily raised her hand, but it was too much to hope that he would wave. She bent her elbow and pretended to be holding the crown of her wide-brimmed straw hat instead.

It was strange enough that Aubrey had offered to keep the store when Lily announced her intention of going to the island. "Offered," perhaps, wasn't exactly the word. He had said, "If you got to go over there, give Sara Eubanks a rest. I'll do it."

Lily bit her tongue to keep from blurting questions about his bees. "Don't you want to ride over there with me?" was all she could think to say.

"I haven't lost nothing over there," Aubrey said, and that ended the conversation.

He had meant it about keeping the store, though, because here she was in the boat, and there he was walking away from the dock. She felt, suddenly, as if she were going on a picnic instead of paying a business visit to Sam Perry about getting some more nets.

At least, she'd told Aubrey that was her reason for seeing Sam. Truly, she could use a few more. Until Sam started making nets for her, Palmetto fishermen had bought cotton twine and made their own. Many still did—Lily stocked twine, too—but others had found Sam's nets were far better than they could make themselves. They bought the nets, and all they had to do was melt down the lead and make the weights. That was done by pouring the lead in a tongslike mold, which Lily could also sell them. She had lumps of lead, too. All in all, Sam had made quite a contribution to the marine supply portion of her business.

Today, however, the nets were only an excuse. Lily's real reason for going to St. Elmo—and it made her feel, secretly, a little excited—was to see if Sam knew anything about a young man named Josh and what he might be doing on St. Elmo.

The inhabitants of St. Elmo could be divided into summer visitors, who rented the low, unimposing beachfront bungalows strung near the water's edge, and those who truly lived there—people who for reasons of economy or eccentricity chose to isolate themselves from the mainland. The latter, Lily had noticed, never complained (as the former did, loud and long) that the sulfur-laden water tasted like rotten eggs, or that you couldn't pick up Arthur Godfrey on the radio, or that two months in the salt air would rust out a car completely.

Sam Perry had lived on St. Elmo all his life. He had seen the island before the developers ever thought of the Elmo House, and he'd tonged oysters out of the offshore beds while the hotel was under construction. He had done the same during the island's brief heydey, and continued during its long decline. Sam not only knew the island, he was unlikely to be surprised by anything that happened there.

Despite some high clouds and a slight stirring in the air, the ride over was smooth. The sun glared on the weathered facade of the Elmo House, with its broken gingerbread trim. Lily tied up at the pier and walked past the abandoned hotel. After a hundred yards or so, the crumbling pavement degenerated into a two-lane sand track.

The track led along dunes covered with sea oats, from which occasional paths meandered to the water. She passed a beached boat lying on its side, its bottom knocked away. A stand of pines marked the tip of the island, and when she passed it Sam's cottage came into view. It was a flat-roofed structure of unpainted concrete blocks. Sam sat on a stool by his front door. The end of the net he was weaving was attached to the doorknob. His small wooden shuttle expertly moved the twine in and out.

A baseball cap shaded Sam's washed-out blue eyes. His face and arms were brown from over seventy summers in the Florida sun. His feet were bare and looked horny and tough. When he saw Lily he touched the brim of his cap.

He brought out a cane-bottomed kitchen chair, settled her in it, and said, "What can I do for you, Miss Lily?"

Lily's business about the nets was easily concluded. That discussion over, the two of them sat gazing across the dunes at the ocean. Lily was almost mesmerized by the heat, the sun on water and sand, the rhythmic movement of Sam's shuttle. Seeing and hearing the waves made the loneliness and confusion of the past months seem insignificant. Sam brought her back: "Have a glass of tea?"

She shook her head. "I been looking for a young fellow who came in the store the other day. I believe he stays over here. His name is Josh."

The shuttle didn't stop while Sam considered. "Don't know the name."

"You may have seen him, though. He's got dark curly hair, dark eyes, wears khaki trousers."

"Could be most anybody," said Sam. "Could be me, if I was forty years younger and had dark eyes."

Lily didn't reply. Sam held out his net to check the meshes. "This boy do you out of some money?"

"Nothing like that. I just need to find him and ask him something."

"Well. . . ." Sam stretched his legs out in front of him. "I haven't seen this boy to know who he is or whether he's named Josh. Does he run a cabin cruiser at all?"

"I don't know. Not that I saw."

"There's a bunch at the other end of the island. Staying in the pine woods, past the lighthouse. Getting eat up by chiggers, more than likely. A couple of outboards and a cabin cruiser. They don't come down this way at all. What they might be up to I couldn't say, but my belief is they think nobody knows they're there."

"They don't know Sam Perry," said Lily.

Sam shrugged. "Makes no difference to me, long as they don't get liquored up and set the woods on fire. But it could be that's where your young fellow is."

"I wouldn't be surprised."

Lily stayed another ten minutes chatting before getting up, stretching, and saying, "Reckon I'd better get along."

Sam rose and touched his cap brim again. As she started across the dunes, he called to her. He looked shrunken and bleached in the glare of the forenoon. "You be careful, Miss Lily," he said. "Don't go after no trouble."

Lily waved as wide as her arm would reach and turned away.

Josh Stands Guard

Murphy had been sitting at the table under the pines, a mug of coffee in front of him, for at least two hours. Josh, Larry, and Amos moved without volition, pretending to work but casting covert glances at Murphy.

The news of the night before—that Elmore had sold them out to the Calhouns and their distribution system was ruined—had shaken them. Amos reacted with his usual bravado, but Josh recognized the tension underneath. Larry asked Josh several times how many Calhouns there were.

Josh himself was trying to think about something besides when he would see Sue Nell Calhoun again. He was appalled that it had become so important to him. He could see that Sue Nell was trouble, had been trouble since she set foot on the boat last night, was likely to be trouble in the future. But that didn't matter in the face of the need she had tapped in him.

I was off balance, finding that body and all, he told himself, knowing it didn't explain how he felt. Under the surface, he had sensed a desperation that touched his own. Maybe that was it. And he could smell and taste her even now, as he went through the motions of cleaning out the mash cooker.

Murphy got up from the table and wandered to where Josh and Amos were working. He beckoned Larry. "You boys sit down."

They gathered around the table with fresh cups of coffee. Murphy leaned on his forearms and surveyed them. "I reckon we all know we got some problems," he said. "This Calhoun bunch has found out about our still. Now, this is what I figure." He swallowed coffee and wiped his mouth. "They don't know where we are, or they'd 've been over here last night. But it could be they'll find out. We been pretty easy on the sentry duty up to now, but we got to tighten up. You boys have your shotguns. We're going to patrol around the clock. You'll do four hours on, eight hours off. And I mean for you to keep your eyes open."

Josh, nodding piously, noticed that Amos and Larry were doing the same.

"What you'll do," Murphy continued, "is stay at the bent tree by the creek where we usually watch. But every thirty minutes you make a circuit of the camp. Anybody that's coming in will likely come by the creek, but we can't take the chance that they'll come overland. We're going to go on making moonshine, which is why I'm only putting one of you on guard at a time. Any questions?"

"Yeah." Larry's voice was hoarse. He cleared his throat and said, "What if we see somebody coming? What do we do?"

"Yell at them to stop," said Murphy. "If they don't, shoot."

The little group was silent. "All right, then," said Murphy. He pointed at Josh. "Get your gun. You're on duty right now."

As he walked through the scrubby undergrowth that bordered the creek, his shotgun under his elbow, Josh felt increasingly morose. Last night Murphy had said they weren't going to make whiskey. Now he'd changed his mind, and it would be much more difficult to see Sue Nell.

It was almost noon. His next duty would be midnight to four in the morning. He was sick of Murphy, sick of moonshine, and sick of this damn island.

He reached the tree that served as their lookout station. Years of gales had bent it, and one branch extended over the creek. Josh hoisted himself into the fork, leaned back against the trunk, and, one leg dangling, turned his thoughts back to Sue Nell.

After a half hour of dead quiet, it was time to do Murphy's prescribed circuit of the camp. Josh jumped down and, feeling nervous for the first time, started through the palmetto and scrub oak, making a wide semicircle. The undergrowth was low and thorny. Josh's hands were sweating, his shotgun felt slippery. Suppose the Calhouns did come? Josh wasn't ready to be killed for Murphy's still. He needed to contact the office to tell them the latest developments but didn't know when he'd get a chance. And suppose Sue Nell had gotten into trouble last night. Suppose her husband had gotten wind of what happened, and came in gunning for Josh?

He had arrived at the creek, half a mile or so from his starting point. Feeling a little easier, he headed back downstream toward his post.

He had almost reached the overhanging tree when he heard the buzz of an outboard motor. It wasn't an unusual sound, and only his unnatural alertness made him notice it at all. After a moment or two, it stopped.

He quickened his pace and soon was back at the tree. He stilled his breathing and listened, but, hampered by the drumming in his ears, heard nothing. He began moving toward the mouth of the creek.

He found the empty boat tied to a bush. The Calhouns had arrived. They could be anywhere. Behind the scrub oak tangled along the creek, lost from sight in the pines, in front of him, in back of him. He stared at the boat, wishing it would disappear, but it rocked at its mooring, undoubtedly real.

He thought of calling out to alert the camp, but discarded the notion. It would warn the intruders, and maybe Murphy, Larry, and Amos wouldn't hear him anyway. He sucked a breath between his teeth and listened again, to nothing.

The only thing to do was get to the camp. He started back upstream. He had gone only a short distance when he heard, or thought he heard, a rustling in the woods to his left. Still heading vaguely in the direction of the camp, he angled toward the sound, moving swiftly in a half-crouch. He heard the sound again.

He stopped to listen, and at that moment saw a blur of motion off to his left. So they were here for sure. They hadn't seen him, or he'd be shot by now. He headed for the spot where the blur had been.

The scrub oak was thick here, head high and choked with vines, and behind it the rustling separated into cautious footsteps. Just one person. They'd sent somebody ahead to look over the situation. Josh ran lightly ahead until he found a thin place in the underbrush, then crouched to wait.

His leg muscles tensed, and when the steps drew even with him he lunged forward. The figure went down without resistance, but the wheeze of lost breath was immediately followed by a thrashing of limbs. Several blows landed around Josh's face and shoulders before he could collect himself. In a moment, though, he had pinned his enemy's hands. He was looking into the eyes of Lily Trulock.

An Encounter

Lily thought she was about to die. She lay on the ground, gasping, her hat knocked off. All she had wanted to do was take a brief and apparently innocent stroll through the woods, so if she saw anything she could go back and convince Woody to look into it. Instead, she was about to meet her Maker. She thought maybe she should say a prayer, and tried to collect herself to think of one. She got her eyes focused and looked at Josh. He seemed shocked. She smelled his sweat.

Her breathing was easier now, and—was it her imagination?—Josh's grip on her wrists seemed to have loosened. She lay still, gathering herself, then snatched her hands free. Using all her strength, she clouted Josh in the face and, when he recoiled, rolled over, scrambled to her feet, and started to run back toward her boat. She looked around for a weapon. A broken branch was lodged head high in a bush, and she grabbed it as she ran.

"Wait," came a low call behind her, and she felt a clutching at her dress. Grasping her branch with both hands, she spun, swinging it like a baseball bat. She saw a sharp twig break the skin of Josh's cheek, saw his hand go up to protect his eyes, saw him stagger as the weight of the branch caught him below the ear. She dropped the branch and ran.

He was slowed by only a few seconds and soon was close behind her again. Lily's chest was burning. "Stop," he said, still in a low voice, almost a whisper. Waves of blackness surged over her eyes. She felt his moist palm close on her arm, and he dragged her to a halt.

"Can't you listen for a minute?" he gasped. "I didn't mean to knock you down. I thought you were somebody else."

She noticed with satisfaction that blood was seeping out of the scratch on his cheek, and clenched her fist to hit him again. "Don't do that," he said, grabbing her wrist. She kicked him in the shin.

Now, he did look murderous. "Goddamn it, ma'am," he said. "Could you just stop doing that?" He looked around. "Now where's my goddamn gun?"

Taking the Lord's name in vain, Lily thought reprovingly. At the same time, she began to feel a little less frightened. He seemed to be saying he didn't want to hurt her, although that could be a trick. Still holding her arm, he marched her back to the place where he'd ambushed her, and picked up his shotgun. "Let's walk along the creek a ways toward your boat," he said. Mindful of the shotgun, Lily obeyed.

When they reached her boat, he motioned her to sit down. She perched on a fallen log, thinking distractedly of how rumpled she must look. What would Aubrey think?

"What are you doing here?" Josh said.

"Fishing."

Josh shook his head. "No fish I know of you can catch in the piny woods, and that's where I found you."

Lily's spirits began to return, bolstered by the unexpected fact that she was still alive. "I hadn't heard that walking in the woods was against the law."

"What were you looking for?"

She shrugged.

He hesitated. "Are you working with the Calhouns?"

The question startled Lily into a short laugh, and the laugh made her feel even better. "I haven't got to make moonshine for a living yet."

Recognition broke over Josh's face. "I know who you are. You're the lady that keeps the store at the ferry landing. You gave me change that time."

She nodded, slightly apprehensive at being recognized.

She saw a muscle jump next to his eye before he said, "Ma'am, let me tell you something. You and me both are going to be in trouble if we aren't careful. I'm supposed to be on guard, and instead of standing here talking to you I should be patrolling. But I think you're up to more than picking up pine cones over here. I want to know what it is."

Lily didn't intend to tell him that she thought he was mixed up in Diana's murder. Why turn his mind to such subjects? Her explanation, when it came, sounded lame even to her. "I saw boats going back and forth. I didn't think anybody lived at this end of the island. I wondered what was going on."

Josh rolled his eyes upward. "Keeping a store must be easier than I thought, if you got that much time to tend to other people's business."

Lily pursed her lips and didn't reply.

"I'm not letting you go till you tell me the truth," Josh said. "We'll just sit here until you're ready to talk or until my guard duty's up. Then you can come back to camp with me, and I'll let my boss tend to you. And I hate to say it, ma'am, but he's a whole lot meaner than me."

He squatted down, selected a piece of pine straw from the ground, and began picking his teeth with it.

Minutes passed. Lily sat on the log, smoothing wrinkles out of her skirt, while Josh gazed into space with every appearance of having forgotten she was there.

A horsefly, buzzing loudly, made a couple of passes at Lily's head. Josh whistled breathily through his teeth. "It's a free country," Lily said. "I've got as much right to be here as you do."

Josh had stopped whistling when she spoke. He resumed without glancing at her.

Lily watched a large red ant making its way across the strap of her sandal. She looked around for the anthill, but couldn't see it. The red ant was a long way from home.

"It was because of that time you came to the store," she said.

Silent now, Josh watched her.

"You acted funny. You were in a big rush, didn't want to stop and talk, just made that phone call and ran off. I thought it was odd. Especially the next day."

"What happened the next day?"

The red ant reached the other side of Lily's foot, started off through the underbrush, and was lost to sight. "I found out Diana Landis had been killed."

"What does that have to do with anything?"

"I don't know. But I do think"—she looked at him boldly—"that that call you made was to the sheriff, about the murder. And I told him so."

"God almighty." Josh straightened. "You told the sheriff about me?"

Lily wondered if she'd just signed her death warrant. "He's my son-in-law. And if I turned up missing. . . ."

Josh stared at her. "What do you reckon I'm doing out here? Can you guess?"

"Since you asked about the Calhouns, I reckon you're making moonshine."

"We need to be secret. We don't need anybody telling the sheriff about it."

"I didn't tell him about moonshining. I told him I thought you made the call about Diana Landis."

Josh seemed to be framing a reply, but before he could make it Lily saw his eyes grow wider, staring past her shoulder. She jumped up, turning in the same motion. A few yards behind her, standing with a shotgun leveled at Josh's chest, stood Sam Perry.

"You put that gun down, young feller," said Sam. His baseball cap was shoved to the back of his head, and Lily noticed that he had put on threadbare tennis shoes. Josh bent and laid his rifle on the ground.

Lily's legs felt wobbly. "Thank God, Sam," she said.

"You and me will get in your boat, Lily," he said, not taking his eyes off Josh.

She went to the boat as Sam slowly made his way across the clearing.

"You don't understand," said Josh. "I didn't get a chance to tell you—"

"From what I see, you been a little bit harsh with this lady here," said Sam.

"Me harsh with her? You ought to see what she—"

"Cast off, Lily," said Sam, stepping into the boat. While he kept the gun on Josh, Lily untied the rope, shoved the boat into the creek, and hopped aboard.

"If you'd let me . . ." Josh began, but the motor started after only one pull and drowned out the rest of his words.

Lily swung the boat around and headed for the ocean, catching only the briefest parting glimpse of Josh's strained face.

An Understanding

"*The Lord bless thee and keep thee,*" intoned Brother Chillingworth. "*The Lord make his face to shine upon thee and be gracious unto thee. The Lord lift up his countenance upon thee and give thee peace. Amen.*"

The scent of flowers hung heavily under the green canopy. The faint snuffling that had been audible when Diana's casket was lowered into the grave next to her mother's was now stilled, and heads bowed for the benediction were raised. People began to murmur to each other in low voices.

Standing in the patchy grass at the edge of the canopy, dressed in her best dress and shoes, Lily tried to compose her mind to say good-bye to Diana. It was difficult. Only this morning, noon really, she had been knocked down and held at gunpoint—or more or less held at gunpoint. Rescued at gunpoint, anyway. And yet here she was at Diana's funeral, exactly where she would have been if nothing had happened.

When she thanked Sam for his help, he said, "I know you, Miss Lily. Once you asked about it, I figured you to come messing around down here. We can't let people get into trouble on St. Elmo, or we'll have the law all over us. No offense to Woody. But the reason we're here, if you follow me, is to be left alone."

He had taken her back to his beached boat and, with a final wave of his hand, he was gone.

If Aubrey had been curious, he didn't show it. When she asked if he minded keeping the store so she could go to Diana's funeral, he ducked his head and said, "All right."

Snapper looked terrible. Perspiring in his black suit, his face the color of dough, he looked transformed from his usual hearty, back-slapping self. When Lily pressed through the crowd to shake his hand and say, "Beautiful service," his grip was lax.

"It was, though, wasn't it?" he said, but she could tell he was thinking about something else.

The Calhouns were there, even the old man, who, his feeble legs bent, had to lean on Sonny. Bo, she noticed, stood away from his family, staring at the grave. Sue Nell—Lily glanced through the crowd again to make sure she wasn't mistaken—Sue Nell was the only Calhoun wife not present.

Isolated from the crowd on the other side of the canopy was a small knot of black people. In the center of the group, Lily saw Pearl standing under her umbrella with her daughter Marinda. The sight of Pearl reminded Lily of the poems, and her unkept promise to show them to Woody. She'd better explain.

As she approached the group, it seemed to loosen. She beckoned to Pearl. "It was a nice service, don't you think?" she said when Pearl got closer.

"Yes ma'am. Surely," said Pearl. Her face was closed, unexpressive.

Maybe she doesn't like being singled out, Lily thought. I've embarrassed her. "I just wanted to tell you I haven't had a chance to talk with Woody about the poems," she said. "I tried, but he didn't want to see them right then. He had just arrested Wesley."

Pearl's hands were twisting a white handkerchief. "Yes ma'am."

Lily looked at her closely. "Is everything all right, Pearl?"

Pearl closed her eyes and nodded.

"Well," Lily pushed on gamely, "I'm going to talk to Woody again as soon as things quieten down. I'll let you know what happens."

Pearl said, "Thank you, ma'am," and turned back to her companions.

Feeling that she had somehow mishandled the encounter, Lily picked through the gravestones toward her car, stopping occasionally to talk with acquaintances. When she reached the Nash, she looked back. The canopy was almost deserted now, the afternoon sun glinting off the bright satin ribbons on the flower arrangements. Pearl stood alone now, near the grave, her head bent. The only one of us who's really sorry to see Diana go, Lily thought. Diana was lucky to have even one person who cared about her that much. A feeling of bereavement that she recognized as having nothing to do with Diana came over her. She got in the car and headed back to the store.

By the time she arrived, her head was once again full of the morning's adventures. A secret moonshine still on the island. Why, she wondered—not for the first time—hadn't she called Woody immediately to tell him? It was, she knew, nothing more than misplaced pride. He hadn't listened to her other suggestions, so why should she hand him a bunch of moonshiners on a plate? Let him find them for himself, the way she had.

But there was another reason she hadn't called. Despite the fact that he'd knocked her down and scared her half to death, she felt a sneaking liking for the man named Josh. He had tried to apologize and had seemed to want to tell her something. He had given the impression of being in some sort of trouble. But, of course, she reproved herself, none of that meant he wasn't dangerous. She had best keep her sympathies under control.

She sent Aubrey back to his bees, and the afternoon wore

on. Schoolchildren bought drinks and candy, messed up the comic books, and left. Passengers for the last ferry idled in, picking up an extra quart of milk, a loaf of bread, a bag of corn meal. Lily yawned. The day's exertions were catching up with her.

The ferry left on its final run. She squinted out the screen door, gauging the weather. It might rain, she told herself, and at that moment the faintest of breezes touched her cheek.

She swept the floor, the door left open for late customers, then put the broom and dustpan in the back room. When she returned, Josh was standing by the door.

He made a conciliatory gesture, looking nervous. "It's all right."

Lily's hands felt cold. She edged along the shelves and picked up a large can of tomatoes. "You do one wrong thing and I'll throw this whole shelf of cans at you."

"Don't start throwing anything." Josh's fingers touched the scratch on his cheek. "I want to talk to you."

"Go ahead."

He edged into the room. "You said the sheriff was your son-in-law. Have you told him about today?"

"I don't have to answer any questions. If you want to tell me something, tell me."

"Well, this is it. I know you think I'm some moonshiner out in the woods. But there's more going on than that. It's real important that you don't tell the sheriff or anybody else about me."

"You ambush me and hold a gun on me. Why should I do what you say?"

The color in Josh's face deepened. "Because I work for the Beverage Department. And it looks like you're about to mess me up bad."

"You're a revenuer?"

"That's what I get called sometimes. And worse things."

Lily almost put down the tomatoes, then changed her mind. "How do I know that's the truth? And why are you telling me?"

"I'm working under cover, so I don't carry identification. You can call the department in Tallahassee and ask them if Josh Burns works for them, and they'll tell you yes."

"That doesn't mean you're Josh Burns."

He shook his head. "No. And I don't know what I could do to prove I am, short of totally ruining my operation, which you're about to do for me."

"What do you mean?"

"If you tell the sheriff, it's going to mess up the whole thing. He doesn't know I'm here. I'm working on a tip from an informer. For all we know, the sheriff may be involved himself. You tell him about us, that lets him know we know. My job is to find out who the head man is. There's a big bankroll behind the operation. It may be somebody the sheriff is friendly with."

Lily knew that Woody was hand in glove with the Calhouns, but the idea that he might be paid off by another group of moonshiners as well was a little disturbing. "Do you think he's mixed up with them?"

"I've got no reason to think so. But just in case, I don't want him knowing I'm here."

Lily thought. The whole thing could be a cock-and-bull story to keep her from turning them in. And yet—she looked at Josh, who was gnawing his lip, his hands in his back pockets. "Have a drink," she said, nodding at the cooler.

He got a strawberry soda and took a long swallow. "Did you make that phone call? The one about Diana?" Lily asked.

Josh sighed. "I was hoping you'd let that go. Yes ma'am, I made the call. I found her body."

"What were you doing there?"

"I was doing my job."

Lily put the tomatoes down. "Does that mean Diana—"

Josh shook his head. "I've told you all I'm going to say. Knowing any more could get you in trouble. You've got to decide what you're going to do."

In the silence that followed, Josh finished his drink and put it in the wooden crate by the cooler. Lily straightened the canned goods, setting them in neat rows. She turned around. "I have one more question."

For the first time, Josh smiled. "I'm getting used to it."

"You said you had an informer. Who is it?"

He shook his head. "If I knew I wouldn't tell you, but I don't know. We got a letter, not signed, saying there was a big new still starting up on the island. I came to see if it was true."

If Josh cleaned himself up, Lily thought, he'd be a fairly nice-looking young man. "All right," she said. "I won't tell Woody—or anybody. Not unless something else happens."

"Ma'am, that's a big relief to me," Josh said.

"My name is Lily. Lily Trulock."

"Thank you, Lily." Josh dug into his pocket. "I've got to make a call, and then I've got somebody to see." He held up a nickel. "I've got the change this time." He waved and was gone.

As she finished cleaning up the store, Lily wondered if she had done the right thing. She locked the cash box and closed the door of the back room. The faint sound of an outboard motor told her Josh must be on his way to see whomever he had to see.

Well, she'd given her word, and she wasn't going back on it. She locked the door and started on her usual walk along the beach.

Tupelo Branch

Josh's hands were shaking as he dialed the operator in the phone booth outside Trulock's Grocery. He had never had to reveal his identity during an undercover job before. That plus the averted ambush last night meant things were not as smooth as they should be. He wondered what Eddie would say. Maybe Eddie would want him to give up and come home. The thought was obscurely comforting, until he remembered Sue Nell. That would mean he couldn't see Sue Nell. But on the other hand he'd be shut of Palmetto, and Murphy, and that damn island. . . . He tapped the glass with his fingers.

Could he trust Lily Trulock? He thought he could. She might be nosy, but she didn't seem foolish or flighty. Keeping a store out here probably got lonely, made her want to keep an eye on other people's business. And now she knew a great deal about his. He wondered what Eddie would say.

As it happened, he wasn't going to find out. "He's long gone, Josh," Louise said. "It's lucky you caught me and not the night boys. I just stayed late to finish typing some reports."

"I wanted to tell him—"

"He did leave a message for you," Louise went on. "Let me see here."

Over the static on the line, Josh imagined he could hear

148

papers shuffling on Louise's desk. "He said if you called to tell you the people upstairs are looking at the situation, but for right now there's no change in your assignment."

"There are some things I needed to tell him."

"About the congressman's daughter?"

"No. Not about that."

"Has the situation down there changed?"

"It looks like the Calhouns are on our trail." He told her about the previous night's events. "Other than that. . . ." He stopped to think. If he could trust Lily Trulock, there was no reason to tell Louise he'd revealed his identity. "I guess that's all," he said. "I got a real mess on my hands here, Louise."

"I'll tell him. Take it easy, Josh."

Take it easy, thought Josh as he wrapped the starter cord around his motor. He gave it a vicious pull and, naturally, the motor coughed and died. Doing it again, more slowly, he went over his mental map of the waterways around Palmetto. Tupelo Branch might be as much as a half hour away. Murphy had been almost amiable about letting Josh come to the mainland—"to check things out," Josh had said. Although Josh knew, rationally, that Murphy simply trusted him more after last night, he still couldn't escape the fear that Murphy suspected something and was setting a trap for him. The smart thing to do would be to get back early. But instead of heading for the island, Josh turned his boat toward the canal.

In fifteen minutes, he swung into the muddy expanse of the Big Cypress River. The water, slightly choppy in the rising wind, had a silvery sheen in the fading light, the banks lined so thickly with trees that they looked black. Soon he'd reach the place where the Little Cypress came in. And down that a ways, on the left, Jones Branch, Bobcat Branch, Tupelo Branch. He opened his motor to full throttle.

A mass of tupelo bushes, laden with long, olive-shaped

berries, stood beside the mouth of Tupelo Branch. Some of the berries floated in the water, bobbing in his wake as he turned the corner. The branch was not wide and was overhung with cypresses, their misshapen knees rearing out of the shallows at the water's edge. He followed several bends before seeing a weathered dock on the right. There were no boats tied to it.

Tears stung Josh's eyes, and he was swept by a disappointment so intense it surprised him. He had never considered the possibility that she wouldn't be there. He slowed and looked at the camp. It was built of rough timber, and stood on pilings against the rising of the river. There was a screened porch along the front, and the roof was tar paper. He could barely make out the privy, down a trail in the back. The place looked deserted.

Maybe this isn't the one, maybe she's on down the creek, Josh thought. He continued for ten minutes and passed another camp. This one had several boats tied up—none of them Sue Nell's bateau—and was brightly lit with kerosene lanterns. Several men sat in the front swatting mosquitos and drinking beer. This could go on forever. I got to get back, Josh thought. He turned the boat around.

When he reached the first camp, Sue Nell was tying up her bateau. She turned as he came closer, standing perfectly still while he drifted in.

"Looky here," she said, her voice tight.

"I said I'd find you."

Standing next to her on the dock, he felt awkward. She was wearing yellow shorts and a white shirt. Her hand, when he took it, felt clammy. "I wanted to see you. Even for a minute," he said.

"No sense standing out here and letting the mosquitos eat us up," she said. "Come on inside."

There were cots on the porch, and roughly built bunk beds inside, one of them made. On an L-shaped counter in a corner stood a camp stove and an upside-down dishpan.

Nearby a pump and a sink. A shelf held canned goods, cotton twine, a mold for making lead weights, a pistol, a tackle box, a straw hat.

"Not a bad place," said Josh, while Sue Nell lit a lantern.

When it was hung on a nail she turned to him. "Why are you looking for me?"

"I can't forget you."

She shook her head. "You've been with women before."

"Not like with you."

Her eyes narrowed. "Who are you? Why are you here really?"

"I told you."

"Not who you are."

"It doesn't matter."

"It does matter."

"I'm a moonshiner."

She shook her head again, more vehemently. "I've been around moonshiners all my life. I'm married to a moonshiner. Something about you isn't right."

"Forget it." Josh moved toward her. "I told you it doesn't matter."

Her eyes, when he looked into them, were full of dread. "This is the last thing I need," she said.

"Me too. Exactly the last thing," said Josh. He touched her hair. "I want to be with you."

When they lay down together and he unbuttoned her blouse, her body was hot to his touch. "You've been in the sun," he said. She shook her head. "Then you have a fever."

"Yes," she whispered, "a fever," and pulled his head down to her.

The thought that he would never be able to let go of Sue Nell was momentary in Josh's mind. Then he closed his eyes and gave himself up to her.

Elmore Takes Sides

"It's over on the island," said Elmore. "I watched the boat the whole way over there."

Some of the recent lines of strain had eased from Elmore's face. His pale eyes were timidly jubilant.

Bo Calhoun signaled to Moody Winchester for another drink and lit a cigarette. "You better be damn sure."

"I'm sure, Bo. I'm positive."

The evening was young at Sal's Roadhouse. The regular customers were drifting in. Hank Williams blared from the jukebox. A breeze gusted in whenever the door opened.

"How did you happen to see the boat?" Bo regarded Elmore closely through drifting smoke.

"I figured where they'd dock. Not too many places you could dock a boat the size of that one. Had to be the mouth of the canal. They come to my place, tried to scare me. Didn't do them no good. When they left, I went by the back roads. I know them roads, Bo. That's why I been such a good distributor for you. I know them roads, and I know who lives there—"

"That's right, you know the roads."

"So I got to the landing before they did. I seen the boat. I hid in the trees. In a couple of minutes, they showed up."

"And you watched them over to the island."

"The south end, Bo. Where nobody ever goes. That's where they went. I could see them easy with their light on."

152

Bo smoked, staring at the scarred wood of the tabletop. Elmore fidgeted with the collar of his shirt. "I hope that's what you wanted to know, you and your brothers."

"That's what we wanted to know."

"I'm glad, because you know what?" Elmore gulped his beer. "I felt bad about the way things have been. It was my mistake. I admit that freely. I should have known when I was well off."

"Yes, you should."

"That's right, Bo, and I want you to know that from now on—"

Bo looked at Elmore for the first time. "From now on, you little son of a bitch, you stay out of my way."

Elmore looked stricken. "But Bo—"

"You stay out of my way, and you don't speak my name or the name of any Calhoun. If I hear you have, I'll kill your ass. You sell me out again, I'll come after you."

"What about being distributor? I got to have some way to live."

"If you want to live, you steer clear of me and steer clear of the moonshine business. You're lucky you aren't dead already." Although Bo's face was stiff, the tone of his voice was almost casual. "Now get the hell away from me, and don't ever come near me again."

Elmore sat still for a moment. Then he rose slowly to his feet. "I know you're mad," he said.

Bo ground out his cigarette. He didn't look at Elmore. "Maybe you'll change your mind," said Elmore. He waited, but Bo didn't reply. "Good-bye, Bo," Elmore said. He turned and left the bar.

Bo smoked another cigarette before going to the pay telephone in the corner. When his call went through, he said, "Give me Sonny." Hank Williams throbbed "Your Cheatin' Heart" while he waited on the line. Finally, he said, "It's over on the island. Tell the boys. We'll go tomorrow."

Revelations

Clouds were banking over the island, and the tide was rising. Lily switched off the weather advisory, which had told her no more than she had guessed from the morning sky. There was a tropical storm in the Gulf, approaching hurricane strength, and it was heading toward Palmetto. The air was moving, the atmosphere subtly changed. Lily hunted for boards to nail, if need be, over the store windows.

While she worked, she thought about Josh and his secret. She was embarrassed to admit to herself how pleased she was that he had told her. When she tried to explain it, the only words that came to mind were *Something Has Happened.*

Lily's life had not been barren of events. But those events had been the ones everybody knew about: marriage, childbirth, illness, quarrels, reconciliations. Good years and bad years. Now, she was involved in something most people never experienced. Undercover operations, secret agents. She had been sought out and taken into confidence. The importance of the trust she was keeping—it was a life and death matter, really—made her shiver with apprehensive delight.

She walked to the ferry landing to take a closer look at the weather. The water was gray, with some swells, but it didn't look too bad yet. Many times storms veered off or lost their strength, and Palmetto, braced for a hurricane, got a hard rain and nothing more.

When she turned back to the store, there was a black jalopy that she didn't recognize parked in front. She saw with a shock that Pearl Washington was behind the wheel. Remembering Pearl's coolness at the funeral, she hurried toward the car.

Although the engine wasn't running, Pearl clutched the steering wheel. "There's trouble at Mr. Snapper's," she said without preamble. "I was hoping maybe you could get the sheriff."

Lily felt her throat close. "What's wrong?"

"He just sits there, drinking whiskey, holding that revolver. Since the funeral he don't talk, he don't go out. He once in awhile peeks out the window, and that's all."

"Couldn't it be he's just grieving for Diana?"

Pearl snorted. "He didn't care nothing about that girl. When she was killed, he didn't hardly bat an eye."

"Sometimes it takes people afterward."

Pearl shook her head. "He's going to kill somebody. I'm scared to be in there with him."

"Pearl"—Lily's mind was racing—"he hasn't shot off the gun or anything, has he?"

"Not yet."

"Knowing Woody, he isn't going to want to go in there and disturb Snapper when Snapper hasn't done anything but sit and drink whiskey and hold a revolver."

Lily saw Pearl's shoulders sag. She's afraid, and she came to me for help, she thought. I can't seem to do anything but let her down. "Let me talk to Snapper first," she said. "Then I'll see what I can do about Woody."

"You shouldn't go in there."

"He won't shoot me." Lily hoped she was right. "I'll meet you there in a few minutes."

She left the *Closed* sign swinging on the door of the store. As she drove toward town, slowly, to give Pearl a chance to reach Snapper's first, Lily wondered what on earth was going on. She'd just talk to Snapper a few minutes and see how bad it was. Maybe she could at least mention it to Woody, despite his lack of interest in anything she had to say. Or maybe Pearl, herself upset by Diana's death, was making more of Snapper's behavior than it merited.

When she rang the doorbell at Snapper's, Pearl answered. "He's still just like I told you. I'll let him know you're here." She climbed heavily up the stairs.

In a few minutes, she returned and said, "I told him you was here. He didn't say a word." She made a vague gesture toward the stairs.

Lily had never been upstairs in Snapper's house, but nerves had gotten the better of natural curiosity, and she hardly noticed her surroundings. At the end of a hall, a door stood slightly ajar. She saw something glittering in the dim crack. It took her a moment to realize that the point of light was Snapper's eye.

"It's just me," she said. He moved back as she approached, and she interpreted this as an invitation to come in.

The windows and blinds were closed, and the air was heavy with cigarette smoke, whiskey, sweat, a faint suggestion of Vitalis. The room was evidently a study, furnished with a desk, chairs, and a bookshelf with a set of encyclopedias. On the walls hung a stuffed marlin and photographs of Snapper with various notable people.

Snapper's rumpled shirttail hung outside his pants, and his hair was greasy and lank across his forehead. Lily had never known him to be less than perfectly groomed. His face looked even more caved in than it had at the funeral, his eyes with the stunned look of a fish flopping in the bottom of a boat. He was holding the revolver, but it hung ignored from his loose fingers.

At the sight of her, his mouth made a parody of his usual grin. "Miz Lily," he said.

"Pearl said you were poorly," Lily said. "I came to check up."

She was close enough now to smell the liquor on his breath. "Poorly," he said. "You can call it poorly, I reckon." He crossed to the windows and peered out between the blinds.

"What's wrong? Is it Diana?"

He let the blind snap back into place and turned to her. "They had to have Di, all right. I should've known it when they had to have Di."

"Known what?"

"That they wanted me."

"Who wanted you?"

He waggled a finger at her. "Folks. The world has got some mean folks."

"But Woody thinks Wesley Stafford killed Diana. If you know different, you should tell Woody."

"No siree. Not Woody. No siree." Snapper's vigorous shaking of his head disarranged his hair even more. He slumped into a chair. "A man has his way to make in the world, Miss Lily," he said. "You try to do it, and they will cut you down and thwart you regardless. They'll hunt you down like you was nothing but a nigger."

The desk was piled with campaign posters with a photograph of Snapper's smiling face and the slogan *Experience in Government*. Lily sat on its edge. "I don't understand."

"I don't understand it myself. It's the way people are."

"If you're in danger, you need protection. I'm going to tell Woody."

Snapper's lip twisted. "No offense, but Woody is about as near useless a lawman as I ever saw."

Lily remembered how, after Diana's murder, she had heard Snapper profess the utmost faith in Woody and Cecil's crime-solving abilities. And Wanda had said he refused to have extra investigative help brought in. Either he had changed his mind drastically or he'd been lying before. Afraid of pursuing the subject, she said "You keep on like this, you'll lose yourself the election."

"If I don't I may lose a damn sight more."

Lily stood up. If Snapper was willing to write off the election he was in more trouble than she could handle. "I'll go now," she said.

He didn't reply at first. After a moment he said, "I won't give them sons of bitches the satisfaction."

"That's right." She moved out of the room and closed the door.

Pearl was waiting at the foot of the stairs. "You want some cake?" she asked.

Sitting at the kitchen table, eating pound cake and drinking coffee while Pearl leaned against the sink, Lily said, "Something is mighty wrong with the congressman."

"My Lord, yes."

"He thinks somebody's after him." Lily chewed slowly, baffled. "I can't figure out what he's talking about. He says they had to have Diana, and now they're after him."

Lily could feel the quality of Pearl's attention change. "He said that?" she asked.

"Yes. I don't understand. But you're right. I'll have to tell Woody."

Pearl put her hands over her face. "Lord, Lord forgive me," she said.

Lily stood up. "What's wrong?"

"My Lord God, I haven't told you everything, Miss Lily."

All of a sudden people want to tell me secrets, Lily thought. Isn't it the strangest thing?

"God forgive me if I'm doing wrong," said Pearl.

"You're doing right. He'll forgive you," said Lily. "What is it?"

"I didn't know it had anything to do with Miss Di," said Pearl. Tears rolled down her cheeks. "Mr. Snapper is mixed up in a moonshine still. I heard all about it in this kitchen. It's over on St. Elmo's Island."

"You can't mean it."

"A big fat man was in this kitchen the other night, telling Mr. Snapper about how the Calhouns had found out about their still and were waiting for them, only Bo Calhoun's wife warned them off. And about how they had dynamited the Calhoun's still."

Lily felt more breathless than she had when Josh knocked her down. "This can't be true, Pearl."

"It's true. But I said to myself, 'Pearl, he's your boss. It's none of your business anyway.' But if it has to do with my girl. . . .'' Pearl sank into a chair and buried her head in her arms on the kitchen table.

Numbly, Lily skirted the table and patted Pearl on the shoulder. "Now Pearl," she said. She squeezed her arm. "We'll figure something out."

"He's scared the Calhouns will find out and come after him," Pearl sobbed. "And you tell me he said they got Miss Diana first."

Her mind racing, Lily continued to rub Pearl's shoulder until her sobs lessened. She searched in her purse for a handkerchief and gave it to Pearl, who said, "I'm so sorry," and wiped her eyes and blew her nose.

"The thing is," said Lily after the two of them were sitting with fresh cups of coffee, "that I can't tell Woody about this. I can't tell you why, Pearl, but trust me there's a good reason."

She stood up. "And I'm going to take care of it. I'm going to take care of it right now."

Driving back as fast as she could go, clouds scudding overhead, Lily gauged the progress of the storm. She could be on the island in twenty minutes after leaving the landing, if the weather held as she thought it would. If the storm hit while she was there, she could wait it out at Sam Perry's. The important thing was to get to Josh as soon as possible. If Snapper was in danger from the Calhouns, Josh was also. And he had to know that Snapper was the man behind the St. Elmo operation. She pushed the accelerator and watched the sand blowing in a fine layer across the road in front of her.

So it came down to the Calhouns and Snapper, Snapper versus the Calhouns. With Diana somehow caught between them. With Diana caught. . . . A thought hit her with such mesmerizing force that she almost swerved off the road. A poem Diana had written danced in her mind. She couldn't quite remember. But didn't it have to do with choosing between her father and someone else? Choosing someone else? Had Diana had to choose between her father and the Calhouns?

She skidded to a stop in front of the store, got out of the car, and ran across the street toward her house. Pearl had said Bo Calhoun's wife warned Snapper's bunch of an ambush. Why would Sue Nell Calhoun do that? She would have to be angry—very angry—with her husband to betray him that way. Lily thought of Bo staring at Diana's grave, and of Sue Nell's absence from the funeral. All Diana's poems, she thought. All Diana's poems were written to Bo Calhoun.

She slammed into the empty house, the screen door banging behind her. She found Diana's composition book on her bedside table and leafed through it, her hands shaking. Here it was:

> *Honor thy father and mother,*
> The Bible tells us to.
> My mother is gone, my father's like stone,
> And I'd rather honor you.
>
> I didn't know it would mean choosing,
> And choosing is hard, it's true.
> But when it came to a decision
> I knew I would have to choose you.
>
> I'd like to have honored my father
> If it hadn't been so hard to do.
> So I won't even try, just let it go by,
> And instead I'll honor you.

That's it, that's it, thought Lily. She chose Bo. And I'll bet she wrote that letter to the Beverage Department. She's the reason Josh is here.

Her hands shaking, she pulled a flowered oilcoth table cover out of a kitchen drawer, wrapped Diana's book in it, and tied it with string. With the package under her arm, she tied a scarf on her head. An old raincoat of Aubrey's was hanging on the coat rack, and she snatched it and put it on. It hung almost to her ankles, the sleeves brushing her knuckles.

The Calhouns will find that still, and then there'll be trouble, she thought. She stopped just long enough to lock the house and then, under a lowering sky, ran down to the landing and her boat.

Lily's Warning

Lily had handled a boat in rough water before. This wasn't the worst, but it was bad. Whitecaps were starting to form, and occasionally one broke against the boat and she caught the spray in her face. Still, she felt excited by the adventure of what she was doing, and not particularly worried. She made steadily for the island, the boat slapping over the waves, the wind in her face making tears form in her eyes.

The need to wipe away the moisture made her turn around momentarily. After blotting her eyes with the end of her scarf, she blinked. Two boats were behind her, just leaving the mainland.

The boats were too far away for her to see who was in them, but Lily had a strong suspicion it was the Calhouns. Nobody without a compelling reason would be on the bay at all. If the Calhouns had discovered that their rivals were on the island, though, the possibility of a hurricane wouldn't stop them.

She turned her face forward again, her confident mood gone. They probably didn't know exactly where the still was. She'd have to get there first. She turned around again and saw, or imagined she saw, that the boats had gained on her a little. She thought she could make out two figures in each boat. Her throttle was open as wide as it would go. She set her face forward.

The wind was increasing steadily, and in its teeth rounding the end of the island took twice as long as usual. The sight of the open Gulf was stunning. Whitecaps all the way to the horizon, both sky and water gunmetal gray.

Lily's arm was stiff from clinging to the tiller. The coast of the island was altered by the rapidly rising tide. Now I just need to find that creek, she thought.

The buzzing of the Calhouns' motors mingled in her mind with the ocean noises. She tried to remember what had led her to the creek before. A break in the grass? But the grass was quickly being inundated by the swirling water. There had been, she thought, an unexpected plant. A yucca plant. And up ahead she saw it, its spiky bulk still obvious above the tide. As she turned into the creek, she looked back and saw that no boats had rounded the point.

It was dark under the pines. The thunder began as she guided the boat along the twisting waterway. A moment later, a drop of rain hit her wrist. She docked her boat where she'd tied up before. Another drop of rain landed in the bottom of the boat near her foot. As she started off through the woods, she thought she heard the motors again.

She ran, heedless of noise. Lightning flared briefly, followed by thunder. She'd have to hurry to beat the Calhouns.

The blond man grabbed her arm before she saw him. She had assumed, without thinking about it, that Josh would be guarding the still as he had before. Being confronted with an angry-looking stranger holding a shotgun was the last thing she had planned on.

"Where you heading?" His voice was harsh.

Lily shook her head, temporarily shocked out of speech. Rain began to patter lightly in the woods around them. "I need to see Josh."

The motors were louder now, unmistakable. The blond man glanced in the direction of the noise, then back at her. "What the hell for?"

Lily was damp with sweat and rain. "Please let me see him."

"I'm taking you to camp." He dragged her along, her raincoat catching on brambles. In a few minutes they entered a clearing where two men—one fat, one with bristly hair—were moving equipment. Relief swept over Lily when she saw Josh nailing boards across the windows of a shed. He turned, and his arm fell slack when he saw her. The other two men stopped work and straightened up.

"Found her in the woods," the blond man said.

Lily wasn't sure what to do. She decided waiting would be a mistake. "The Calhouns are coming," she blurted out. "They left right behind me."

The little group converged on her. "What do you mean?" the fat man said.

"They're on their way. You can hear the motors."

Nobody said anything. The only sound was the rain and wind in the trees.

"Sure you can," the fat man said.

The blond man, who still held her arm, said, "I did hear something a while back, though."

"They'll be here any minute," said Lily.

The bristly-haired man said, "Oh God," and looked around at the trees.

"She asked to see Josh," the blond man said.

The fat man squinted at her. "What's your name?"

"Lily Trulock."

"From the grocery store?"

"Yes."

He looked at Josh. "You know her?" Josh nodded, looking numb. The fat man indicated the shed. "I want to talk to both of you. Get on over there."

Lily and Josh had almost reached the shed when a sharp crack split the air followed immediately by the glare of lightning. Lily turned and in the weird illumination saw the bristly-haired man grab at his stomach. Josh pulled her toward the bushes beside the shed, and from their cover she watched the blond man aim his gun and fire at the moving figure she could see through the trees. The rain began to pour in sheets. Through it and the thunder, Lily heard the screams of the man who'd been shot. The fat man, more nimbly than she would have supposed, grabbed a gun and crouched behind the table.

"Oh Christ. Oh Christ," Josh said. "They shot Larry."

"It's the Calhouns," Lily said. "I came to warn you. And to tell you—"

Suddenly Josh scrambled from their hiding place toward the wounded man who was lying, quiet now, on the ground. Startled, Lily waited a second, then followed. Amid the gunfire, Josh took Larry under the arms and Lily took his feet. They dragged him into the shed.

The drumming of rain on the corrugated tin roof almost drowned out the muffled thuds of the shots. "Larry," said Josh.

Larry's eyes flickered, unfocused. "Hey . . ." he said, and Lily saw his mouth fill with blood. His head fell to one side, and the blood oozed onto the dirt floor.

"Oh God," said Josh. He put his head to Larry's chest, then felt his pulse. When he turned to Lily, his eyes looked large and very black. "He's dead. Let's go," he said. They slipped out the door and into the trees behind the shed.

Several times during their frantic progress through the woods Lily thought of letting Josh go on without her. Her legs felt rubbery, and she seemed to be constantly watching his back disappear. At the point she'd decide she'd lost him, though, he would turn and wait. Her heart labored, and she wondered if this were how Aubrey felt when he had his attack. She was no longer conscious of her streaming hair under the wet scarf, or the ground squelching under her sandals, or anything but the tightness in her chest.

Josh halted abruptly in front of her and held up his hand for caution. She crept up behind him and followed his gaze through the trees. The edge of the creek was almost in front of them. A little way down was a dock where several boats were tied. Standing on the dock, wearing foul-weather gear and holding a shotgun, was Lester Calhoun.

"We can take my boat," whispered Lily, nodding downstream.

They went more slowly now, fearful of alerting Lester. The trees were thrashing in the wind, and the storm noises drowned out any possibility of knowing if the gun battle continued. Finally they reached her boat. Several inches of water had collected in the bottom. Lily found an old bait can and bailed while Josh started the motor.

Once they were on the bay the boat wallowed helplessly. Waves slapped the bow and sprayed in their faces, and water slopped over the sides. Lily bailed furiously, knowing it was doing no good, knowing it was useful only for keeping her mind and body occupied.

The only advantage was that the chance of pursuit was slim. The boat reared like a bucking horse, and she closed her eyes until it was obvious they would stay upright.

Although they were keeping as close as possible to land, Lily could barely see the coastline through the gray downpour. She strained to see if they were making progress. They were trying to round the point. How long had they been opposite that bulking line of trees? Lightning flashed, and she lurched forward, instinctively ducking her head.

She looked at Josh. His arms bulged as he fought to control the boat, and his face was taut. He had only his thin, short-sleeved shirt and khaki pants against the gale. He'd felt kindly toward the man who was killed, she thought, and realized that until that moment she had forgotten that she'd just seen someone die.

The seas grew worse. As the boat was slammed from wave to wave, Lily began to fear that it would break up. She had heard of such things and seen splintered boards washed up on the beach after a storm. Once she had found a

Thermos bottle with coffee still in it. She had poured the coffee out on the sand. "You have to pull in!" she yelled at Josh. "We won't make the mainland!"

Josh nodded. As they neared the shore Lily recognized the terrain. They had come further than she thought. Up ahead was the Elmo House. "The hotel!" she cried.

They washed in to the beach on boiling waves. Lily jumped out in knee-deep surf to pull the boat in. The tide had risen so high that the abandoned pool in front of the hotel was filling with sea water. She tied the boat to one of the posts that held the broken-down fence.

Josh was shaking out a tarpaulin. "Get the stuff out of the boat!" he shouted.

Frenziedly, Lily took everything that came under her hand—seat cushions, another tarpaulin, a tackle box, the bait can—and put them on the beach. Rummaging under the bow, she saw something lying half in the water. What's my tablecloth doing here, she thought, then remembered. Diana's poems. She flung the package into the pile with the rest, then helped Josh lash the tarpaulin over the boat.

Battered by rain and nearly blown off their feet by wind, Lily and Josh labored up to the Elmo House carrying the things from the boat. Rainwater poured over the sagging floor of the hotel porch.

The screen door of the Elmo House was loose on its hinges, but the heavy wooden front entrance was boarded over and nailed shut. Josh shoved it and kicked it. It shuddered and held firm.

"Wait," said Lily. There was a way to get into the hotel. She knew that, because there had been scandals from time to time about high school girls getting pregnant there. She followed the veranda around the side of the building and found a broken window with its protective boards swinging free. She called Josh and, carrying their burdens, they climbed through.

They were in a large, high-ceilinged room with a fireplace. This was the dining room, she thought, and fleetingly remembered a long-ago meal—it might have been fried chicken—and a sunny room with white tablecloths. Debris was piled in the corners, wallpaper hung in strips, and the floor was covered with a fine layer of sand. A gust of wind rattled the windows. The building creaked.

A puddle was forming around Lily's feet as her raincoat shed water. The windows rattled again. Through them, she saw a pine branch hurtle through the air and hit the side of the building with a thud. She wondered how the Elmo House would stand up to a hurricane.

Out of the Storm

Josh sank down with his back against the wall and rested his head on his knees. Lily, still dripping, watched him. The things they had brought from the boat were in an untidy heap under the window. She took the tarpaulin and a cushion and proffered them to Josh. He glanced up and shook his head. She unfolded the tarp. "Better wrap up in this."

He made a tent around his shoulders with the stiff canvas and closed his eyes. Lily sat down a few yards away, but despite her exhaustion she felt jumpy. She was cold, too. Water dribbled from her hair to her neck, sliding underneath the raincoat collar. She shivered and got up.

"You got any matches?" she asked.

Josh shook his head without opening his eyes. She searched the tackle box. Hooks, sinkers, corks, line. A pair of pliers for extracting hooks, a minnow net, a bait rag, an out-of-place assortment of nails and screws. Underneath it all, a box of matches. She held them up. "Found some."

There was a wadded paper bag and a few candy-bar wrappers among the broken beer bottles in the corners. She collected these and pulled strips of damp and mildewed wallpaper from the walls. That might start a fire, but she needed wood to keep it going. She walked into a dark and drafty hall. Across it, another door opened into what had been the hotel lobby. Tall front windows looked out on the furious surf. Her boat, Lily could see, was still right side up, although now tossing on the ever-rising seas. Pigeonholes that had once held mail for guests gaped empty on the walls, and in the center of the room, listing on a loose leg, stood a rickety ladder-back chair, its cane bottom rotted away.

Josh looked up when she reentered the dining room dragging the chair. "Firewood," she said.

After several false starts, they coaxed a smoky, wavering flame into life in the stone fireplace. They crouched in front of it, feeding in pieces of wood Josh had broken off by knocking the chair against the floor. Despite the constant groaning and creaking of the building and the lashing rain, Lily began to relax. Some color, she noticed, had come back to Josh's face, although he still looked drawn. "I'm sorry about your friend," she said.

"Oh"—Josh pulled the tarp closer around him—"he wasn't my friend. None of them was my friend. But he was nicer than the others." He gazed into the fire. "Thanks for trying to warn me."

"I'm sorry it happened the way it did." Then she remembered. "I didn't come over here to tell you about the Calhouns, anyway. It was something else. I found out that Snapper Landis, the congressman, put up the money for your still. I was coming to tell you that."

Josh stared at her. "How do you know?"

She told him about her conversation with Pearl and Snapper's strange behavior, and went on to her deduction that Bo and Diana had been lovers.

"That's right. I knew that already," Josh said.

"You did?"

"Sue Nell Calhoun told me." He shifted, looking uneasy. "I know her."

Lily waited for him to continue. When he didn't, she said, "I figure Snapper had Bo's still blown up, and Diana found out about it. To get even, she wrote to the Beverage Department and turned in her own daddy."

He shrugged. "Maybe."

"I'm positive. She wrote a poem about it." Lily unwrapped the oilcloth package. Diana's composition book was dry. She found the place and handed it to him.

His eyes moved over the lines. " 'When it came to a decision, I knew I would have to choose you,' " he said. He leafed through the other pages, occasionally stopping to read. "She was a wild little thing, wasn't she?"

"Wild. Miserable. And nobody really cared about her but the colored maid."

"And ended up caught in a net, a big old catfish trying to eat her fingers." Josh handed the book back, and she rewrapped it in its covering. He rubbed his eyes. "I expect you're right about her sending that letter. If we get out of here alive I can check it."

The fire flickered. Although it was only late afternoon, the room was darkening as the intensity of the storm increased. "Bo Calhoun must have cared about her," Josh said after a pause.

"I don't know. Diana told Pearl he almost hit her once." She looked at him curiously. "What does Sue Nell say about it?"

He shook his head and didn't answer.

In a moment, he got up and left the room. She heard him climbing the stairs. When he returned, he had some loose boards under his arm. "Found them in one of the rooms," he said. "Maybe left over from when they shut the place up." He knelt and fed the fire.

Lily watched him. "How did you get into this line of work?"

He sat back. "Didn't want to farm. Hurt my daddy, but there it was. Finally got on with the Beverage Department."

"It doesn't bother you?"

"What?"

"I don't know"—Lily waved her hand—"work with people, then turn them in."

"They're breaking the law. And I'll tell you the truth.

Some of them are all right, but some are the sorriest folks you ever saw. Take that Murphy I been working for. And the blond fellow, Amos. Those are two mean sons of guns."

How was the store, Lily wondered. And her house. And Aubrey. He would see the boat was gone and think she was dead. Maybe she would die and never get home. Would he be sorrier if she died, or if she lived? "Are you married?" she asked.

Josh grimaced. "Nope."

"You must be twenty-five. Why not?"

"I'm twenty-six. I reckon I didn't love anybody enough."

"Maybe it doesn't take so much."

He set his chin. "It does for me."

"You've been in love?"

He kept his eyes steadily on the fire. "I'm in love now."

It was the answer Lily had expected. "With Sue Nell Calhoun," she said.

Josh nodded.

Lily breathed out between her teeth. "Well, aren't you in trouble."

"I'm in trouble," said Josh. "I'm sitting here worrying about how she's getting through this storm, instead of worrying about how we're going to. She's up at a fish camp."

"On Tupelo Branch? She'll be all right, I imagine. Of course, the river will rise. But she's been through this all her life, you know."

Josh looked slightly happier. "That's right."

Lily felt light-headed. She hadn't eaten since breakfast, but the feeling was less hunger than a dizziness that came from having too much to take in. The dizziness and Josh's confidences made her reckless. "My husband doesn't talk," she said.

He frowned. "Ever?"

"Oh, he says something now and again. Hello, good-bye. He goes out and keeps his bees. I don't see him much. He's been this way since his heart attack."

"He's scared he's going to die, probably."

"Everybody's scared they're going to die. That's no reason to act like you're already dead."

Lily was surprised at the anger in her voice, but Josh didn't seem disturbed. "That's right."

"I didn't give him a heart attack. Why stop talking to me?"

"I don't reckon he's thought about that. He just doesn't feel like talking, so he doesn't talk."

Lily was silenced by this simple logic. Her face felt warm. She had never complained to anybody about Aubrey's behavior before. She felt guilty but relieved. At least John hadn't acted as if he thought it was anything shameful. She rested against one of the boat cushions, watching the fire. In a few minutes, she was asleep.

The Still Destroyed

Bo Calhoun's ax bit into the oak barrel, and mash adulterated with rainwater belched out, mixing with the mud on the ground. It swirled near the heavy shoes of his brother, Sonny, whose body lay half under the table in the clearing. The roof had blown off the shed, and Purvis and Lester huddled next to one of the walls, close by Larry's mud-spattered body.

Bo hacked at the barrel until it was little more than splinters. He took one of the iron rings that had bound it together and flung it, as hard as he could, into the trees. Then he stood, swept by rain and wind, leaning on the ax, his shoulders heaving.

The clearing was filled with wreckage. Twisted pieces of metal, disconnected copper pipes, broken glass littered the ground. The camp stove was lodged in a bush. The lantern had been shattered, but its top half still hung from a branch, swinging crazily in the gale.

Purvis, his head bent against the rain, left his place by the shed wall and ran to Bo. Tentatively, he put his arm around Bo's shoulders. Bo gave no sign of noticing. Purvis pulled at him. "Come on over here, Bo!" he bawled in Bo's ear.

Bo allowed himself to be led to the shed where he crouched with his brothers, only slightly out of the wind. He wiped his nose with the back of his hand. "I'll kill those sons of bitches," he said. He looked at Larry's body. "We only got one. And they got Sonny." He rounded on Lester.

174

"Why the hell did you leave the dock? You let them get away!"

"There was all kinds of shooting. And I heard something," said Lester. "I was trying to do it right. It's my fault Sonny got killed." His face collapsed, and his heavy body shook.

"No, old buddy." Bo shook his brother's shoulder. "That fat one made a lucky shot, is all. But I'm going to fill his gut full of lead. Don't you worry about that." He looked around. "Where's my gun?"

Purvis handed it to him. It was wrapped in a raincoat. "It's loaded," he said.

Bo felt in the pockets of his foul-weather gear. "I got plenty of shells." He leaned toward Lester and Purvis. "You stay here till the storm lets up, and take Sonny's body home. Leave my boat at the dock. When I've found them and killed them I'll come back for it. If they show up here, shoot them."

Purvis's face was ashen. "Where you going, Bo?"

"They can't get off this island. I'm going to find them." Bo drew the hood of his jacket tight around his face. With his gun under his arm, he left the clearing. He didn't look back at his three brothers.

A Long Night

When Lily woke, the room was almost completely dark. A few embers still glowed in the fireplace, and, by their light and the last murky illumination at the windows, she could see Josh slumped asleep under his tarpaulin, his head on a boat cushion.

There was some wood left. She tore off more wallpaper and with it teased the embers back into flame. When the fire was burning again, she walked to the windows and looked out.

At the sight she froze, amazed. The ocean had risen nearly to the edge of the veranda; waves broke and rolled across the weathered boards. Spray mingled on the windows with the incessant rain. The only way they could reach the boat now, presuming it was still there, was swim for it. Lily clutched her raincoat around her. How long could the old hotel stand this battering?

She looked in the opposite direction, up the ridge on whose slope the hotel stood. The white sand and sea oats, the overlooking row of pines, all were neatly obscured by dark and rain. Something was moving across the sand. A branch blowing, perhaps, or a beach towel from someone's clothesline.

Her attention was distracted by a loud groaning of timber, then a cracking sound, and she turned to see that one of the supports of the veranda roof had given away, and the roof was swaying toward the water. She backed away from the window, less from the instinct to protect herself than from unwillingness to see more.

Behind her, she heard Josh scramble to his feet. "What the hell was that?" His voice was hoarse with sleep.

"The porch roof is about to fall down. And we've got water on our doorstep."

He came and looked out. "My God."

The sound of glass breaking, followed by a heavy thud, came from the back of the hotel. Josh said, "Jesus Christ, what now?" The sound of running feet echoed down the hall. Before either of them could move, Bo Calhoun appeared in the doorway, pointing a shotgun.

Bo's eyes darted around the room, then came to rest on Josh. "I'm Bo Calhoun. My brother's dead," he said. "Are they here?"

Josh shook his head.

Bo walked forward. There was an intensity in his face Lily had never seen there before. "You were at the still. I saw you," he said to Josh. "You're one of them. You know where they are."

"I don't."

The look on Bo's face frightened Lily. She said, "Bo—"

He glanced at her. "They got Sonny, Miss Lily."

"I'm so sorry."

He frowned. "I don't know what you're doing here, but you shouldn't be around. Because this boy has got to tell me where his friends are. There's two others and him left alive. They blew up my still, and they killed my brother."

"But you can't—" said Lily, and stopped. To tell Bo that Josh was a revenue agent would make no difference. Bo had been brought up hating the Beverage Department worse than the devil. And, even if he knew, he probably still wouldn't believe that Josh didn't know where Murphy and Amos were. Looking at Josh's face, set in stolid lines, she wondered if he did know.

"Now, I'll tell you what we're going to do," Bo said. "We're going to wait out the storm right here. When it lets up, you're going to tell me where their little hidey-hole is."

"I don't know."

"If you don't tell me when I ask you next, which is going to be when we're about to leave here, I'll shoot you. First in one leg, then in the other leg. First in one arm, then in the other arm. You'll tell me."

"You wouldn't do that, Bo," said Lily.

Bo didn't take his eyes off Josh. "You've wandered into the wrong place this time, Miss Lily. You stay out of the way. This is between me and him."

There's more than that between the two of them, if Bo knew it, thought Lily, remembering Sue Nell. The two men stood motionless, like figures balanced on a seesaw. "You two come over by the fire," said Bo.

Lily and Josh sat at the hearth, and Bo stationed himself a little distance away, leaning against the wall. Lily looked at Josh, wondering what was going on in his mind. His face was expressionless, his manner completely calm. He obviously wasn't going to try to bait Bo. Considering the dangerous mood Bo was in, Lily decided to follow his lead.

Bo, on the other hand, seemed to want to talk. "No sir, those boys won't get anywhere tonight. They'll be waiting for us tomorrow." He rested the shotgun on his knees. "I plumb tore up your still," he said to Josh.

When Josh didn't respond, he continued. "I went the whole length of the island in this weather. When I saw the fire and your boat and I broke in here, I thought sure to God I had them. But I'll get them." He turned to Lily with a weird grin. "Won't I, Miss Lily?"

"I reckon so."

"Sure I will." He ran his hand over the gun's stock, then glanced at Lily again. "You put your nose into the wrong people's business this time, didn't you?"

"Looks like it."

"Better stick to selling nets and molds. Even if they are the sorriest ones I've ever seen."

Lily was stung. "You knew that mold was uneven, and I gave you fifty cents off and a lump of lead."

"That's right. You told me about the mold, but you didn't tell me about the net."

"What do you mean?"

"I was just looking at it this afternoon when I was cleaning out my boat to come over here. There isn't a square mesh in it. I could make a better one myself."

"Sam Perry made those nets."

"Maybe old Sam's hands are starting to shake."

He's saying that out of pure hateful meanness, Lily thought, and she had her mouth open to protest further when a long, agonizing crack sounded from outside, ending in a crash of tumbling wood and shattering glass. The fire danced crazily as wind gusted through the room. The three of them were instantly on their feet. Through the broken windows the collapsed remains of what had been the porch roof were dimly visible.

Bo's gun was leveled. "You stay right there," he said. "This whole damn place will fall in before I let you get away. Sit down."

Lily sat down, feeling a surge of despair. I'm in a building that's collapsing, in the middle of a storm, with a man who's going to kill me, she thought. If he kills all the others, he'll have to kill me. She bowed her head.

The fire fluttered and died. In a moment, a beam of light shone out. "You aren't going to catch me in the dark," said Bo. He directed the flashlight at the tarp Josh had been wrapped in. "You're going to get that over the windows some way, and then you're going to rebuild the fire."

Bo held the light, and Lily and Josh fastened the tarp over the windows, nailing it in place with nails from the tackle box, using the heel of Josh's shoe as a hammer. All of it seemed vague to Lily. Fear and exhaustion were battling inside her, but a new emotion, complete indifference, was becoming stronger than either. When the fire was rebuilt, she put her head on a cushion and closed her eyes.

That she was able to sleep seemed strange, but waking at intervals through the long night, stirring to see Bo sitting alert, his eyes glowing in the dying fire, and Josh drowsing, leaning on his elbow, she knew she would soon lapse again into unconsciousness.

What woke her at the gray beginnings of dawn was not a sound, but the absence of sound. The absence had continued, she realized drowsily, for some time. Her eyes opened at the realization of what it was. There was no sound of rain, no roaring wind. She heard the surf, but only as it was in a good, clean blow. She blinked. The hotel was still standing. She sat up, rubbing her eyes.

"That's right, time to go," said Bo, and her tiny impulse toward hope withered. She looked at Josh. He gave nothing away, but she sensed a wariness in his manner that hadn't been there the night before. "Let's pack up," said Bo.

Wearily, she bent to gather the few items that had seen them through—the tackle box, the cushions. When she picked up the oilcloth-wrapped package that was Diana's book, Bo said, "Wait a minute."

She stopped. He waved his gun at the package. "What's that?"

She shook her head, not knowing what to say. "It's nothing."

A triumphant look came over Bo's face. "You don't want me to see it?" He held out his hand. "Give it to me."

Lily handed it over. Grinning, he undid the loosely knotted string with one hand, keeping the gun trained toward them with the other. He unfolded the oilcloth and, taking the book, let the wrapping drop to the floor. When he glanced at the book, his face went slack.

The instant Lily noticed the change in Bo's expression, she felt Josh, standing near her, spring toward him. Bo went down heavily. Diana's book, knocked from his hand, slid across the floor.

Without thinking, Lily went after it and picked it up, then turned to see the two men struggling. Josh seemed to have the upper hand, but Bo was fighting insanely, and Lily could sense his desperation. The gun, locked in Bo's hand, swayed between them.

Lily took the tackle box and, gritting her teeth, brought the corner of it down hard on Bo's temple. When Bo's eyes unfocused, Josh grabbed the gun and backed off, aiming it at Bo. Bo stumbled to his feet, said "I'll kill you!" and started for Josh.

The report of the gun reverberated through the room, and Lily wondered if the noise would do what the storm couldn't—bring the hotel down. Although the walls shook, they stood. It was Bo who fell, a burst of red at his shoulder.

Lily sensed Josh taut beside her. She saw the gun sight still at his eye, his hand tense on the trigger. "No!" she screamed. "You got him once!" She shoved at Josh's arm, and the next deafening shot thudded into the wall.

She stood looking at Josh, her hands pressed to her mouth, while he lowered the gun. Her fingers, she realized, were wet with tears. She ran and knelt beside Bo.

He was staring at the ceiling. He didn't seem to know who she was. "Di's book," he said. "She wrote those." He took a long breath and fainted.

She looked at Josh. His face was working. "He was right," he said. "It's time to go."

On the Mainland

The trip back to the mainland seemed, to Lily, both unreal and exquisitely clear, with the unreal clarity her dreams sometimes had. Josh wading out to the boat in waist-high water and pulling it to the front steps, the two of them struggling to get the semiconscious Bo on board, Josh pulling frantically when the motor wouldn't start at first—these images had no power to touch her. During the ride, the bay almost playful now in its roughness, she gazed at the coast as if she had never seen it before. Absentmindedly, she blotted sweat from Bo's forehead as, his hands tied, he thrashed in the bottom of the boat. She saw the ferry landing loom in front of her with no more emotion than she would feel at the sight of a familiar tree stump.

Green glass, glittering in the emerging sun, was strewn in front of the store where a carton of empty coke bottles carelessly left outside had been tossed by the wind. Otherwise, there was no damage she could see. The Nash was pulled up where she'd left it.

"I'll drive you to town," she told Josh, digging in her raincoat pocket for the keys.

He looked at her closely. "You're sure you want to?" When she nodded, he didn't protest.

The surf was boiling up close to the edge of the road, foam scudding across in front of them, but in the sun it no longer seemed threatening. The ocean side of the pavement had a nibbled-at look, and Lily thought they'd have to do some road work before next year.

Woody's car was in the parking lot when they pulled up at the jail entrance in back of the courthouse. She went ahead and found him while Josh helped Bo out of the car. Woody didn't look happy to hear her story, and when she turned to Josh and said. "This is Joshua Burns from the Beverage Department," his jowl lines deepened.

He glanced at Bo and said, "I'll call the Doc." As he turned to the phone, he said, "Daddy Trulock was mighty worried."

Then, Lily was left alone. Josh talked with Woody, and long distance to his office, and with Woody some more. She sat, more or less forgotten, on the bench in the outer office. She tried to call her home once, and the store once, but there was no answer at either place. The doctor came in to look after Bo. Josh stuck his head out of Woody's office and asked Loyce to get Tallahassee again. Cecil walked in, carrying a doughnut and coffee. There was, it occurred to her, something she wanted to ask.

"Cecil," she said.

He turned politely. "Ma'am?"

I must look a fright, Lily thought, the first time she had thought about it. She gathered her dignity. "I want you to do me a favor."

Cecil nodded in a way that said he thought he'd best humor her. "What is it?"

"I want to see the net. The one that killed Diana."

Cecil looked like he wanted to defer to Woody. But Woody was closeted with Josh. "Please, Cecil," said Lily in a tone that meant there was no "please" about it.

He led her into a side room and unlocked the metal drawer of a cabinet. He took out a bag, opened it on a table, and pulled out the net. It was stained yellowish brown from the canal water. She held it up to the light and looked at the even squares that formed the meshes. She ran the finger over the dull gray lead weights hanging around the bottom. Then she thanked Cecil and turned away.

Eventually, Loyce took pity and brought her coffee and a sweet roll, and shortly after that Josh emerged. "You didn't have to wait. The sheriff is going to loan me a car," he said. "Thanks, though." He bit off the words abruptly.

"What's the matter?" she said.

"Come on out here."

They stood in the parking lot while Josh told her that Tallahassee was not anxious to bother Congressman Snapper Landis with a moonshining charge. "They're looking for every kind of way to get out of it. At this point, they don't even want to talk to Pearl. And all your son-in-law will do is fold his hands and say what a fine man Snapper Landis is, and how good for Palmetto."

"Sounds like him."

"Maybe they'll catch Amos and Murphy and they'll tell on him. Otherwise, I went through all of this for nothing."

Lily could think of no comforting words. The sun beat down. Tomorrow it would be as hot as ever. "I found out something while I was waiting," she said. "I saw the net Diana was killed with. It's Bo Calhoun's net."

Josh took her arm. "Are you sure?"

"Yes. I wouldn't recognize the net itself, but I recognize the lead weights. He made them with the mold I sold him. It was uneven on one side, and I gave him fifty cents off. And the meshes are square and even. I knew Sam Perry wouldn't make a bad net."

"You mean Bo killed Diana?"

Lily's mouth tasted bitter when she heard the hope in his voice. "I mean his net killed Diana. He kept it in his boat. You can figure it out, if you want to think about it—"

"No." Josh's fingers dug into Lily's arm. "Bo must have done it. He got mad with her, she was giving him trouble—"

"Then why would he tell me I sold him a bad net? Why bring it up?"

"Just . . . just to throw us off. To make us think that—"

"No. Somebody made another net, quick, and put it in the boat before he missed it."

Josh pushed her away. "You're crazy." His voice was tight. "Just shut up about it. Don't say any more." He got in the sheriff's department car and skidded out of the parking lot.

Lily sagged against the Nash for a few minutes, searching for the strength to drive home.

Lily and Aubrey

Lily's kitchen looked strange to her. The yellow walls, the oilcloth-covered table, the Mixmaster on the counter were like relics from another age. She knew instinctively that the house was empty.

The note was on the table, weighted down by the sugar bowl, and she had started the coffee in the percolator before it caught her eye.

"Lily, I know you left because I wasn't paying attention," Aubrey's scrawl read. "If you find this, it means you have come back. I'm glad you came back. The Coast Guard is looking for you. I will be home soon. Love, Aubrey." She smiled slightly, biting at the knuckle of her thumb, and took the note with her and left it on her dressing table while she took a bath.

Soaking in the tub and shampooing her hair made her feel better. As she dressed, she wondered what she should do about Josh and her theory about Diana's murder. His anger had made her feel bereft. I kept him from killing Bo, too, she thought. But that might make him madder. That I saw what he almost did. She sighed. Maybe a cup of coffee would help her think.

Preoccupied, she wandered into the kitchen and stopped short. Murphy and Amos were sitting at the table.

The two men had a battered air. Murphy's shirt was smeared with grime. A bloody handkerchief was tied around Amos's hand, and his lank blond hair was filthy. In his good hand, he carried his gun.

"We're looking for Josh," said Murphy.

"He isn't here."

"He coming back?"

"Not that I know of."

Murphy stretched exaggeratedly. "Reckon we'll wait and see, then."

Amos seemed less inclined to be tolerant. He walked toward Lily, towering over her. "We're going to find that double-crossing son of a bitch," he said. "We'll teach him about taking off in the middle of trouble."

Wait till you find out how much you really were double-crossed, Lily thought. She walked past Amos to the percolator. Her lack of fear surprised her. Perhaps she had simply been through too much to be afraid. "I made coffee," she said. "You want a cup?"

"Might as well," said Murphy.

Suddenly, as she got mugs from the cabinet and napkins from the drawer, Lily was angry. She had had about enough of this. Enough of people waving guns around, and wanting to know where other people were, and shooting at each other. Enough of people walking in unannounced with no manners at all. Enough of people who threatened to hurt her.

Without stopping to consider what she was doing, she unplugged the percolator and loosened the top. Then she turned and flung it at the two men.

The coffee spurted out in a brown, steaming sheet, and as she headed for the door Lily saw Murphy put up his hands and Amos duck. Then she was outside, the screen door slamming behind her, running down a track that led away from the beach and into the woods.

The screen door banged again. Her only advantage, a slight one, was her knowledge of the woods. She also knew where she was going even if she didn't know exactly why.

The storm had torn limbs from trees and strewn them in the way. She dodged over them. Behind her, she could hear Amos and Murphy pounding through the underbrush. She tried to put on a burst of speed in order to get away from them and hide, but they were too close. She began to smell the creek. It wasn't far now.

"Aubrey!" she called as she burst into the clearing. There was the apiary, the white hives standing amid waist-high vegetation. And—yes—there was Aubrey, wearing his mesh bee veil, his smoker in his hand, at the farthest hive. He looked up at her call.

"Lily," he said. "I called the Coast Guard. I thought you—"

Amos and Murphy ran out of the woods behind her.

"Who are you?" Aubrey said.

"They're moonshiners, Aubrey, and—"

"Shut up," Amos said. He motioned with his gun. "Get out of the way, old man."

Aubrey came closer. "You got some quarrel with me and my wife?" He stopped next to the hive nearest them. Gray wisps drifted out of the tip of the metal smoker.

"Put that thing down," said Murphy.

"This?" Aubrey held up the smoker. "All right." He bent and placed it on the ground. As he straightened, he bumped the hive. "You hear that?" he said.

The air vibrated with angry buzzing. "They're upset," said Aubrey. "They didn't like that storm. They're upset as they can be." He drummed his fingers on the hive, and the buzzing grew louder.

"Stop it," said Amos.

Aubrey thumped the hive again, and the sound grew in volume.

"I said—"

"What I could do," said Aubrey, "I could pick that thing right up and throw it at you. Now, you could shoot me, but maybe I'd rather be dead than covered with mad bees.

Because, I guarantee you, they're looking to sting." He placed a hand on either side of the hive.

"Don't do that," said Murphy.

"I'll kill you right now," Amos said.

"Before I'm hit, this hive will go over," said Aubrey.

"I said don't," said Murphy.

"Then you get out of here, and leave me and my wife alone. We got no quarrel with you."

Murphy and Amos looked at each other. The buzzing was insistent. They turned and walked back into the woods.

Aubrey removed his veil and mopped his head with a handkerchief. "You would have hurt your bees," Lily said.

"I thought you were dead," said Aubrey. "I want to know what happened."

Back to Tupelo Branch

Cecil's motor was more powerful and his boat was bigger than Josh was used to, but by the time he reached the Big Cypress he had adjusted. The local law had been very accommodating, letting him borrow a car and a boat. He suspected it was so he wouldn't look too closely at the sheriff's ties with the Calhoun brothers. What did it matter anyway? Josh thought. With Sonny dead and Bo wounded, the Calhouns would be out of commission. And even if Snapper wasn't prosecuted, his still was in ruins. Amos and Murphy would be picked up eventually. The people of Palmetto would have to find other sources for corn liquor. Josh didn't doubt they would manage to do that.

He tried to keep his mind on these matters and not think about anything else. He wished he hadn't been that way with Lily. He wished she hadn't. . . . He concentrated on watching the river and trying to gauge how much it had risen during the storm.

The tupelo bushes were half under water when he turned into Tupelo Branch, and muddy water extended into the swamp. When he reached Sue Nell's camp, he saw that the dock was under water, so he tied his boat to the front steps. She stood on the screened porch watching him, her arms folded.

"You're all right," he said as he climbed up.

"It wasn't that much. Just a big blow." She cocked her head to one side as he opened the door. "You look like hell."

"I don't want to talk right now."

I know I shouldn't, but I can't help it, thought Josh as he kissed her. Grief and confusion fell away in his intense longing for Sue Nell. I have to, he thought, his hands gliding over her body. Never to do this again. I couldn't stand it.

Afterward, he played with her loosened hair as they lay in the bunk. Now, he thought. "I have to tell you something," he said. "I shot Bo."

Her body went rigid against him. She sat up and searched his face. "Is he dead?"

"No. But he's in jail. I'm the law. He and his brothers killed a man."

"The law?"

With anguish, he felt her shrink away. "Revenue agent," he said. "I'll tell you something else. Diana Landis was killed with Bo's cast net."

Her lips moved for a moment before she said, "How do you know?"

"Lily Trulock recognized the weights on it. She knows they were made with Bo's mold."

She shivered. He saw goose bumps on her arms, a golden hair sprouting from each.

"I thought maybe Bo killed Diana with that net," he said. "That's what I thought at first."

"And now?"

"You tell me."

Her lips twisted. "I thought you knew all along," she said. "I thought that's why I was going to bed with you, because you knew. When you told me that about finding her body. . . ." She gave a coughing laugh. "I thought that's what this was about."

"It isn't."

She got up, and he lay without moving and watched her dress. Finally he said, "When I got here the other night, you'd just put the new net in Bo's boat?"

She nodded. "I worked all day and all night. I wove that

damn thing faster than you've ever seen. I took his mold, and I made more weights. He hardly ever fishes. I figured he'd never know."

"He took it out when he went to raid the still on the island, and he saw it was made sloppy. He told Lily."

"I don't know why I took his boat to go see Diana," Sue Nell said. "I guess because it was fancier than my bateau, to go to her fancy boat in. I wanted to tell her she couldn't have Bo, no matter if he wanted to go or not.

"I found her all tied up. Hog-tied, like a present. I reckon that preacher boy did that. I saw how easy it would be to whip the hide off her, and I got Bo's net, and twisted it, and hit her with the weights. You know, she never thought I'd kill her. She begged me not to break her nose."

"And you kept on."

"I kept on."

"Why?"

"I hated her, with those damn poems. I hate him, too. He would have gone, eventually. I hate them both."

Josh folded his hands behind his head. His eyes barely moved when Sue Nell picked up the pistol from the shelf. "Tell me something before you shoot," he said.

"What?"

"Did you ever care about me at all? Really want me at all?"

"No."

Josh closed his eyes. He didn't wince when the gun went off.

Saying Good-Bye

Lily sat behind the counter reading the *Saturday Evening Post,* waiting for the mid-morning ferry. Three days had passed since the storm, which had not after all been a hurricane. "Close to a hurricane, though," Lily had told Aubrey. "Close as I care to get."

The weather was hot again, but not as hot as it had been before. Something in the air suggested fall. The primary election was in less than two weeks.

Someone walked in. She looked up, saw that it was Josh, and put her magazine down. He was dressed in a dark blue suit, with a white shirt and a tie. His hair was newly cut. He looked like a stranger.

"I was hoping you'd stop in," said Lily.

"Sure I came. I had to say good-bye."

"Going back to Tallahassee?"

"For right now."

He walked around the store, glancing at the shelves, opening the drink cooler. "Have yourself a coke," said Lily. He opened one and dug into his pocket. "My treat," she said.

He took a swallow. "Glad they got Amos and Murphy."

"That was something, wasn't it? The Coast Guard people spotting them right after they came out of the woods?"

"Murphy's screaming about Snapper being involved in the still, but I'll bet Snapper gets out of it yet. And wins the election." He shook his head.

"Something I wondered," said Lily.

"What?"

"When Bo was looking for Murphy and Amos. Did you know where they were?"

"Guessed. There was a little inlet where Murphy moored that cabin cruiser. It was a protected place. I figured they were on board, waiting it out."

"More comfortable than the Elmo House, probably. I think they're going to tear it down, now." She adjusted the lid on one of the candy jars. "Wesley's daddy came and took him back to Montgomery. I reckon they won't be putting money for a youth worker in next year's church budget."

He finished his drink and put the bottle on the counter, then rocked back on his heels, jingling the change in his pockets. "Well," he said.

Lily cleared her throat. "I'm sorry about Sue Nell."

Josh looked away. "What you don't know. I thought she was going to shoot me. I didn't even care. If I had thought she was about to kill herself—"

"I guessed that."

"She must have hated me. You couldn't do that to somebody unless you hated him."

"Maybe she didn't know what else to do. Maybe she didn't want to kill you, and that was the only choice she had."

"Maybe."

Josh leaned against the counter. "How are you and your husband doing?"

"All right, I guess. He talks more." She paused. "I wish you the best."

He colored. "I'm sorry I got mad with you. I didn't want to believe what you were saying."

"I know."

"And thank you for stopping me, not letting me kill Bo Calhoun."

"Everybody was wrought up."

They were silent. Then he said, "You ever get to Talla-hassee?"

"Not too often. You never can tell, though."

"If you do, you call me up."

"Sure I will. And if you ever get back here—"

"Sure." He stood up. "I'll see you, then."

"Have a good trip back."

The door closed behind him. Lily sat running her finger down the coke bottle he had left on the counter, making designs in the moisture on its side. When she heard the ferry's engine, she took the bottle and put it in the rack. She wiped the ring of moisture from the counter and stood waiting to greet any customers.